Praise for Karis

Sit. Stay. Love.

"A cute and fun romance set in a small town. Great main characters that are easily relatable."—*Kat Adams, Bookseller (QBD Books, Australia)*

"This is a sweet romance about two lovely people growing together and falling in love as they help the people and animals around them."—*Rainbow Reflections*

"This is an easy romance to read. It's not overly fraught with angst, but there are some light drama to keep the plot moving forward. The obligatory separation of the leads near the end of the book didn't feel eye roll worthy, because, though dramatic, it was set up almost from the beginning of the book. I loved the characters, pacing and plot of this book. Very recommended."—*Colleen Corgel, Librarian, Queens Public Library*

Love on Lavender Lane

"Gentle romance, excellent chemistry and low angst…The two MCs are well defined and well written. Their interactions and dialogue are great fun. The whole atmosphere of the lavender farm is excellently evoked."—*reviewer@large*

"[*Love on Lavender Lane*] was very nearly my perfect romance novel. Lovely human beings for main characters who had fantastic chemistry, great humor that kept me smiling—and even laughing—throughout, and just enough angst to make my feel it in the heart. And a cute doggie, too!"—*C-Spot Reviews*

Seascape

"When I think of Karis Walsh novels, the two aspects that distinguish them from those of many authors are the interactions of the characters with their environment, both the scenery and the plants and animals that live in it. This book has all of that in abundance…"—*The Good, the Bad and the Unread*

Set the Stage

"I really adored this book. From the characters to the setting and the slow burn romance, I was in it for the long haul with this one. Karis Walsh to me is an expert in creating interesting characters that often have to face some type of adversity. While this book was no different, it felt like the author changed up her game a bit. There's something new, something fresh about this book from Walsh."—*Romantic Reader Blog*

"Both leads were well developed and you could see them grow as characters throughout the novel. They also had great chemistry. This slow burn romance made a great summer read."—*Melina Bickard, Librarian, Waterloo Library (UK)*

Tales From the Sea Glass Inn

"A wonderful romance about starting all over again in middle age. Karis Walsh creates an affirming love story in which relatable women face uncertainty and new beginnings, with all of their promise and shortcomings, and come out whole on the other side."—*Omnivore Bibliosaur*

"*Tales from Sea Glass Inn* is a lovely collection of stories about the women who visit the Inn and the relationships that they form with each other."—*Inked Rainbow Reads*

Love on Tap

"Karis Walsh writes excellent romances. They draw you in, engage your mind and capture your heart…What really good romance writers do is make you dream of being that loved, that chosen. Love on Tap is exactly that novel – interesting characters, slightly different circumstances to anything you have read before, slightly different challenges. And although you KNOW the happy ending is coming, you still have that little bit of 'oooh—make it happen.' Loved it. Wish it was me. What more is there to say?"—*Lesbian Reading Room*

"This is the second book I have read by this author and it certainly won't be my last. Ms Walsh is one of the few authors who can write a truly great and interesting love story without the need of a secondary story line or plot."—*Inked Rainbow Reads*

You Make Me Tremble

"Another quality read from Karis Walsh. She is definitely a go-to for a heartwarming read."—*Romantic Reader Blog*

Amounting to Nothing

"As always with Karis Walsh's books the characters are well drawn and the inter-relationships well developed."—*Lesbian Reading Room*

Sweet Hearts: Romantic Novellas

"I was super excited when I saw this book was coming out, and it did not disappoint."—*Danielle Kimerer, Librarian, Reading Public Library (MA)*

"Karis Walsh sensitively portrays the frustration of learning to live with a new disability through Ainslee, and the pain of living as a survivor of suicide loss through Myra."—*Lesbian Review*

Mounting Evidence

"[A]nother awesome Karis Walsh novel, and I have eternal hope that at some point there will be another book in this series. I liked the characters, the plot, the mystery and the romance so much."—Danielle Kimerer, Librarian, Reading Public Library (MA)

Mounting Danger

"A mystery, a woman in a uniform and horses…YES!!!!…This book is brilliant in my opinion. Very well written with great flow and a fantastic plot. I enjoyed the horses in this dramatic saga. There is so much information on training and riding, and polo. Very interesting things to know."—*Prism Book Alliance*

Blindsided

"Their slow-burn romance is a nuanced exploration of trust, desire, and negotiating boundaries, without a hint of schmaltz or pity. The sex scenes are sizzling hot, but it's the slow burn that really allows Walsh to shine...the deft dialogue and well-written characters make this a winner."—*Publishers Weekly*

"This is definitely a good read, and it's a good introduction to Karis Walsh and her books. The romance is good, the sex is hot, the dogs are endearing, and you finish the book feeling good. Why wouldn't you want all that?"—*Lesbian Review*

Wingspan

"I really enjoy Karis Walsh's work. She writes wonderful novels that have interesting characters who aren't perfect, but they are likable. This book pulls you into the story right from the beginning. The setting is the beautiful Olympic Peninsula and you can't help but want to go there as you read *Wingspan*."—*Romantic Reader Blog*

The Sea Glass Inn

"Karis Walsh's third book, excellently written and paced as always, takes us on a gentle but determined journey through two women's awakening...Loved it, another great read that will stay on my re-visit shelf."—*Lesbian Reading Room*

Worth the Risk

"The setting of this novel is exquisite, based on Karis Walsh's own background in horsemanship and knowledge of showjumping. It provides a wonderful plot to the story, a great backdrop to the characters and an interesting insight for those of us who don't know that world...Another great book by Karis Walsh. Well written, well paced, amusing and warming. Definitely a hit for me."—*Lesbian Reading Room*

Improvisation

"Walsh tells this story in achingly beautiful words, phrases and paragraphs, building a tension that is bittersweet. As the two main characters sway through life to the music of their souls, the reader may think she hears the strains of Tina's violin. As the two women interact, there is always an undercurrent of sensuality buzzing around the edges of the pages, even while they exchange sometimes snappy, sometimes comic dialogue. *Improvisation* is a true romantic tale, Walsh's fourth book, and she's evolving into a master romantic storyteller."—*Lambda Literary*

Harmony

"This was Karis Walsh's first novel and what a great addition to the LesFic fold. It is very well written and flows effortlessly as it weaves together the story of Brooke and Andi's worlds and their intriguing journey together. Ms Walsh has given space to more than just the heroines and we come to know the quartet and their partners, all of whom are likeable and interesting."—*Lesbian Reading Room*

By the Author

Harmony

Worth the Risk

Sea Glass Inn

Improvisation

Wingspan

Blindsided

Love on Tap

Tales from Sea Glass Inn

You Make Me Tremble

Set the Stage

Seascape

Love on Lavender Lane

Sit. Stay. Love

Liberty Bay

Love and Lattes

Mounted Police Romantic Intrigues:

Mounting Danger

Mounting Evidence

Amounting to Nothing

University Police Romantic Intrigues:

With a Minor in Murder

Visit us at www.boldstrokesbooks.com

LOVE AND LATTES

by
Karis Walsh

2023

LOVE AND LATTES

ISBN 13: 978-1-63679-290-3

This Trade Paperback Original Is Published By
Bold Strokes Books, Inc.
P.O. Box 249
Valley Falls, NY 12185

First Edition: January 2023

Credits
Editor: Ruth Sternglantz
Production Design: Stacia Seaman
Cover Design by Jeanine Henning

LOVE AND LATTES

CHAPTER ONE

B onnie James unlocked the outer door of her café, shutting it carefully behind her before she crossed the tiny foyer and opened the second door. All along Sumner's Main Street, she saw other people entering their small businesses, taking advantage of the early morning hours before customers appeared. Stolen, quiet moments to prepare for the day ahead, breathe in the tranquility of peaceful solitude, reflect on the day's goals and life in general…

Those people didn't have twenty-three hungry cats waiting for them.

Bonnie waded through a sea of tuxedoes, gingers, and calicos, all of whom were vying for a piece of real estate on her calves to either rub against or claw, depending on their individual inclinations. Parade master to a chaotic swarm of felines, she walked down the hallway with slow, measured steps to avoid stepping on a cat or an unexpected hairball. She smiled at the cacophony of meows—ranging from raspy yowls to tiny mews—as they trotted along with their furry tails waving like banners in the air, trying their best to trip her up.

When she had first come up with the idea to open a cat café, she had quickly realized that the typical retail space wouldn't be suitable for her needs. The logistics of trying to fit cats, the paraphernalia associated with keeping so many of them, a human kitchen, and room for her customers into a single place had seemed impossible until she had stumbled across this two-story house. On the edge of the small Washington city's business district, its block had recently been rezoned from residential to commercial, and the four-bedroom, two-bath home had seemed perfect to her.

She could clearly remember the feeling she had when she stood in the empty living room for the first time, imagining the bare hardwood floors covered with cat toys and small tables, filled with customers drinking coffee and playing with kitties. Falling in love and adopting them into forever homes. She had been blissfully caught up in the dream of her café and had significantly underestimated the amount of work involved in just the basic day-to-day running of the place.

Fortunately.

If she had been more realistic in her understanding of what she was taking on, she might never have gone ahead with her plans and would have instead walked out of this house and run back to her old, predictable job.

She dropped her sacks of groceries on the kitchen counter and then went into the small downstairs bedroom behind the kitchen that she used as the cat pantry. The shelves were piled with cat food and tubs of litter, and the floors were covered with umbrella stands full of feathery wands and baskets of felt mice—all the delicate toys that would be destroyed in minutes if left with the cats overnight. Some of the cats were distracted by the toys and started batting at ribbons, giving her a little more freedom to move as she piled a tray with cans of food and stacks of stainless steel bowls. She carried the tray into the main room of the café and scattered the bowls around, plopping scoops of wet food into them as quickly as she could. After some brief squabbling, the cats settled into their preferred feeding arrangement, with a few pairs sharing meals and the others zealously guarding their own space.

Bonnie paused for a moment and caught her breath as she watched the breakfast being greedily consumed. In her first week, she had tried to feed like she did with her personal cats at home, lovingly scooping out each meal and arranging it on the dishes in an appealing mound. The region below her knees had become a battleground as cats fought to be closest to her and first to get fed. She had learned that the faster she raced across the room and haphazardly dumped food into bowls, the faster the cats were to find their places and start eating in relative peace.

She sighed and headed up the old-fashioned and steep staircase to continue feeding. She had a dozen cats who got along relatively well and had the run of the house—minus the kitchen and cat pantry—overnight. The smaller upstairs bedroom was home to three senior cats and two younger ones that were too timid to handle the more roughshod downstairs group without supervision. Bonnie fed the five—a much more relaxed experience than the frenzy below—and shut the door again. She'd let them out when customers started to arrive, but they had their quiet space for eating and sleeping.

Lastly, Bonnie carried the nearly empty tray into what had been the house's main suite. She held it under one arm as she opened the door and unlatched the baby gate, scooting past the eager kittens that came to greet her. She shut the gate behind her and sank onto the floor, letting the kittens climb on her lap and try to scale her shirt and get to her hair. She cuddled each of the six one at a time, giving them a quick once-over and nuzzling their soft fur.

Definitely her favorite part of the day.

She reluctantly set the last kitten on the ground and scooped their food into shallow bowls. She had originally planned to live in this suite, that she'd move herself in after the three kittens she'd had in here temporarily were adopted, but that first litter had been replaced by another.

And another and another.

Until it had become the official kitten room. She had started by letting potential adopters come see the kittens, then had begun to bring them food and drinks while they were visiting. The experience had become so popular that Bonnie had turned it into a more structured event, and now, although the kitten room wasn't accessible to everyone, it could be reserved for a limited number of customers for afternoon tea. The kittens received good socialization for short periods of time and were seen by potential adopters, but without the higher traffic of the downstairs public areas. The concept had been a good business decision for the café, and the money those afternoon teas generated made it more cost effective for Bonnie to rent a small house nearby rather than living here.

Bonnie pushed herself off the floor. She would gladly have spent her entire day here, but she had a long list of chores waiting for her. Funny how she had imagined that the main duty of a cat café owner would be playing with cats or reading books with them on her lap. Her pre-café self had been woefully naive. She wouldn't change a thing, though, even now when she was all too aware of the reality of this lifestyle, and even when knowing that the next chore on her list was to clean about a billion litter boxes.

She tidied the kitten room, cleaning up spilled water and straightening rumpled bedding. The space would be more thoroughly cleaned and set up closer to the tea guests' arrival, but for now she just made sure the kittens would be comfortable. She closed them in their room and opened the other door so the quiet-room cats could roam the house, then went back downstairs with her tray of empty food cans and dishes.

She finished her morning chores on autopilot, cleaning boxes and hiding away some of the more bedraggled—but much loved—cat beds. The cuter, less frayed ones remained scattered around the room, ready for daily cat naps. She filled the dishwasher with cat bowls and started it before checking the whiteboard to make sure she was ready for the rest of the day.

She did her best to ignore the note reminding her that this was a nail trim weekend. What was an ordeal with one cat was overwhelming when she was facing hundreds of tiny claws. Still, it was a necessary chore since bleeding customers didn't tend to be happy ones.

She had just changed into a clean shirt and washed her hands when Isa Rosario arrived. Some of Bonnie's favorite patrons were students from nearby colleges. Away from home for the first time, a lot of them missed the regular interactions they had with family pets, and they'd come from as far away as Seattle and Tacoma and spend hours in the café. And like Isa and her afternoon counterpart, Jerome, who were both students at nearby Pierce College in Puyallup, they could be counted on to immediately fill any staff openings Bonnie advertised on the café's bulletin board.

"Did you get them?" Isa asked eagerly, in place of a normal greeting, as she walked into the kitchen and hung her coat and backpack on a peg by the door.

"I sure did," Bonnie said, gesturing toward the totes on the counter, two of which were stuffed with fresh rhubarb. She doubted many others would be as excited about the farmer's market find as she and Isa were, but they tended to see everything in terms of cat adoptions. The more specialty items the café offered—especially using fresh and local produce—the more regular customers they would attract. And the more customers interacted with the cats, the more likely they were to fall in love and adopt. "Not as much as I wanted, but we're still early in the season. We'll sell out before noon every day, I'll bet, and I'm going to Ben and Daisy's farm Thursday to get more."

"Yum," Isa said, peering in the bags. "Oh, good, strawberries, too. Are you making your upside-down cakes? We'll need to save at least seven for the Kitten Tea customers today, and one for me. I suppose one for Jerome, too, or he'll be a grouch all day. Your usual?"

"Yes, please," Bonnie said as the whirlwind that was Isa bustled out of the kitchen again. Bonnie could hear her chatting with the cats as she ground coffee and prepped the counter area before the morning rush.

Bonnie put three trays of Danishes she had prepared the night before into one of the two industrial-sized ovens. The house's original kitchen had been large and open, but with outdated and small appliances. Bonnie and her contractor had spent hours working out the best way to fit the enormous fridge, dishwasher, stoves, sink, and island into the room. The kitchen no longer felt spacious, and it was a tight squeeze to walk around in it, but Bonnie had plenty of surface area for cooking and prepping food.

Isa came in and set Bonnie's usual hazelnut latte with almond milk on the island next to the pile of freshly washed and chopped rhubarb.

"Did you decide on your project yet?" Bonnie asked as she mixed flour, sugar, and cinnamon in a bowl. She sprinkled a handful on the bottom of the pie shells to help seal the crust and keep it from getting soggy from the fruit's juices, then mixed the rest with the rhubarb. Isa had just started her spring term. Luckily, she had another year to go, because Bonnie was going to hate to lose her once she graduated.

Isa leaned her hip against the counter. "Well, if you don't mind, I thought I could use the café. I could track expenses and revenue for a month, and it would be interesting to factor in the way specialty offerings like the teas impact profits. I know it's a lot to ask…"

"Nonsense. I don't mind at all," Bonnie said, putting aside her personal discomfort at the idea of anyone besides her seeing how little she made at the café. But it wasn't as if Isa was going to call Bonnie's parents and tell them about her miniscule profit margin. Not that Bonnie cared what they thought, of course. She was a grown-up and had made her own choices.

So there.

She smiled at the juvenile mental image that phrase put in her mind, complete with hands on hips and tongue stuck out.

"You're a business student, so it's only reasonable for you to use your workplace as a real-life example for your studies," she continued. "I'm glad to help, but be prepared for the rest of your class to feel sorry for me once they see the data. Of course, that might not be a bad thing. If they come here after for coffee, they'll probably leave good tips."

Isa laughed along with her, but with a shake of her head. "You might not make a fortune doing this, but the café means more than money. You're providing a service to a small community by creating a place for people to gather together. And rescuing cats and finding them homes is so important. That's part of what I want to cover in my project—how small businesses can have value beyond profits."

"Well, if you can convince your professor of that, I'll have you come meet my family and you can work your magic on them," Bonnie joked. Isa grinned at her and went back to the counter, leaving Bonnie to firmly put all thoughts of nonexistent profits out of her mind and concentrate instead on filling trays with baked goods.

Mornings at the café were too hectic for her to have time to think beyond the next batch of scones, anyway. She alternated between making pastries and helping Isa with customers when the lines got long. Twice, she was called out to the front to chat with potential adopters about particular cats and the adoption process. She had just started laying out bread for lunch sandwiches when Isa poked her head around the door.

"Nancy's here," she said. "She just parked out front."

Bonnie groaned. Nancy Caine. Her nemesis. Or her best friend, depending on how many cats she was trying to smuggle into the café. "Lock the door," she hissed.

"With customers here? Isn't that a fire hazard or something?"

"Never mind. I'll take care of it." Bonnie replaced the cap on the mayonnaise jar and set it on the island. "Is she carrying anything? A crate? A cardboard box?"

Isa left, then reappeared. "No, just a purse."

"Big enough to hold cats?"

Isa shrugged. "One, maybe. Two if she really squished them in."

Which meant she probably had three in there. Bonnie hurried through the café and made it into the foyer just as Nancy was coming through the outer door. She blocked the entrance to the café.

"We're closed," she said.

Nancy peered around her. "You might want to tell all those people who are sitting at your tables and eating your bagels."

Bonnie ignored the comment and pointed at the bag hanging from Nancy's shoulder. "New cat carrier?"

"Silly Bonnie. It's a purse. I thought I'd buy myself something pretty."

"Liar. One, it's ugly," Bonnie said. She was somewhat envious of Nancy's effortless elegance. Her silvery-gray hair was cut in a sharply angled bob, and she was wearing one of her signature bold outfits, with a black and white striped shirt and a well-tailored, flashy red jacket. She somehow managed to look chic and not like a character from a children's book. The bulky lime-green purse definitely did not convey the same stylish look.

"Two," Bonnie continued, ignoring Nancy's mock insulted expression, "I can see your wallet and keys in your jacket pocket instead of in this new purse of yours. Three, it's wriggling."

Nancy sighed and unclasped the bag, lifting a large ginger cat out of it. "You can always see right through me, Bonnie. Fine, I can tell that you won't keep him, but I thought it was worth a shot. Poor old guy was abandoned by his previous owner, and I thought he would have the best chance of finding a new home if he came to your café. He's such a sweetheart."

Nancy rested her cheek against the cat's head. Bonnie thought that was a brave—but potentially unwise—move, given the cat's expression of supreme annoyance. She wasn't sure whether his grouchiness was a result of his general personality or the fact that he had been recently stuffed in a purse.

"You have to stop bringing me cats until I can get some adopted. I'm full."

"I know, I know," Nancy said, her bright smile returning as she thrust the cat into Bonnie's arms. "Just hold him for a moment, while I buy myself a croissant. Then I'll take him back home."

She pushed past Bonnie and into the café, calling out a greeting to Isa and leaving Bonnie standing in the foyer with her arms full of irritated cat. She scratched his chin and heard the rumblings of a throaty purr. She sighed and pushed the inner door open with her hip, following Nancy into the café.

What was one more? Might as well make it an even two dozen.

CHAPTER TWO

Taryn Ritter ended her call and leaned back in her chair. She now knew far more about turtle anatomy and physiology than she had ever cared to know. She was probably more qualified than most local vets were to discuss turtle diseases and skin conditions at length. Where were the party invitations when she needed them? She had hours of potential conversation topics at hand, especially if the other party guests were amphibian aficionados.

Maybe it was best that her evening plans included a glass of wine, a good book, and no other people.

Taryn looked at the crowded walls around her, trying to decide where she'd hang the photo of Timmy the Turtle. She kept her office furnishings subdued—not sleek and modern, but sparse and unadorned—so the framed pictures surrounding her were the stars of the show. Her clients didn't come to see her style or to let her tastes influence them. They came here because they wanted weddings as unique as they were, and she had a reputation for being the best. She didn't judge. She didn't ask *Why?* even when the question was on the tip of her tongue. She simply listened to what her clients wanted and did her damnedest to make their dreams come true.

In reality, most of the requests she received were familiar

to her after nearly a decade of running her wedding planning business. People arrived with ideas they thought were so far out of the box they were in a different room from it altogether, but often they were asking for what she thought of as *another skydiving wedding* or *another wedding with everyone dressed as woodland fairies.*

She never, never let on to her clients that she had already planned a similar ceremony. In a world full of traditional Cinderella weddings and cookie-cutter dessert bars and appetizer stations, the people who sought her services wanted to feel special. To feel understood and celebrated for who they were.

She had carefully curated the showcase of wedding photos on her walls and in her sample books to make sure they felt specific enough to keep from being repetitive. She was always able to find some aspect of the wedding to photograph on the day that would feel fresh and one-of-a-kind. It wouldn't do to have potential customers flipping through page after page of interchangeable pictures of couples at baseball games or waterskiing in formal wear.

Taryn checked her inbox and saw that the anticipated email from Washington State University's vet school had arrived. She downloaded the attached forms. Although few requests had the ability to surprise her anymore, occasionally something would happen while planning an unconventional wedding that caught her off guard, as had happened in her most recent project.

Lydia and Brent—the soon-to-be Campbell-Smiths—had come to her with their dream of getting married at the aquarium. Easy-peasy. Taryn could plan that in her sleep, even if they wanted to say their vows while scuba-diving in the big tank, or have the wedding party photographed while holding starfish, or have a seal walk them down the aisle.

Their one request? They wanted their pet turtle to be the ring bearer. Taryn had fought to keep her face neutral when they told her about Timmy—she didn't judge, after all, she just wanted her clients to be happy. She had thought the idea was a little odd, and Timmy certainly qualified as the unique touch that would set their wedding photo apart in her displays, but she hadn't expected what an ordeal it would be to bring an outside animal into the aquarium.

Finally, after more calls, texts, and emails than she could count, to more turtle experts than she had realized existed in the United States, she had the required forms in hand that would allow Timmy to be wheeled down the aisle in a flower-bedecked cart pulled by the reluctant—but long-suffering—best man.

She had needed this win, this sense of accomplishment no matter how ridiculous the subject matter, before she met with her new potential clients this afternoon.

Her assistant, Angelina McHale, opened the door and came in the office without knocking. Angie never knocked.

"Well? Did you fix it?" she asked. "I have Timmy on the line, and he's very worried that he won't be able to be in the wedding. He's been pacing all day—he's made it about halfway across the living room."

Taryn smiled. "How long have you been waiting to use that one?"

"For days," Angie said, wiping tears of laughter from her eyes. While Taryn had seen this issue as a problem that had to be solved, Angie had treated the whole turtle episode as a source of endless amusement. "Actually, it's Lydia on the phone. What should I tell her?"

"Let her know I'll be sending an email with all the details. I have a form her vet will need to fill out, and Timmy will have to be examined by the aquarium's vet. There's also a quarantine period, which shouldn't be a problem. I doubt he spends his evenings hanging out in bars with other turtles."

"Let's hope not," Angie said with a derisive snort as she left the office. "Wouldn't want him to have more of a social life than you do."

She shut the door before Taryn could comment on her insubordination. Not that she would, however. She was sure the phrase *I'm your boss—you should treat me with respect* would be met with more gales of laughter than a Timmy joke.

Angie's comment might have some truth to it, but still... Rude.

Angie was one of her former clients. She had come to Taryn's office with her soon-to-be second husband—now her second ex-husband—asking for help planning a wedding on a fishing boat in Puget Sound. The concept was basic, but Taryn had planned the hell out of that wedding. Angie and her ex finished their vows as the boat passed under the Narrows Bridge, with a sunset in the background that was now the subject of one of Taryn's absolute favorite display photos. The waters had been rougher than expected, and Taryn was sure she'd been about as green as the bridge, but the wedding was perfect.

Unfortunately, the marriage, for the two months it lasted, was *not*. When Angie showed up at the office soon after her divorce, Taryn saw her in the reception area and assumed she was there to demand a refund since her marriage failed, but instead Angie informed her that she was there for a job. Taryn agreed to try the arrangement, partly because she felt a twinge of guilt that one of her weddings hadn't ended with a happy ever after, and partly because she didn't think Angie would take no for an answer.

She'd had her doubts since Angie's past work experience was limited to being a cashier in a grocery store since she was eighteen—not to mention that Taryn wasn't even looking for an assistant—but after only a few hours, she had no idea how she had managed as long as she had without her. Angie was brash and had no sense of boundaries, but she charmed Taryn's clients and whipped the office into shape like a no-nonsense nanny dealing with a disobedient child.

Taryn had a great mind for details, but her level of focus on whatever event was immediately in front of her usually meant she ignored everything else until it was completed, and Angie happily stepped in to sort out whatever slipped through the cracks while Taryn was preoccupied with her latest wedding.

Taryn heard a burst of Angie's laughter through the door, and she quickly shoved her turtle notes into a drawer and hurried out to the front of the office. As much as she appreciated Angie's unrestrained personality as a counterpoint to her own sometimes tightly wound nature, she wasn't sure her new clients would feel the same.

"...so the marriage didn't last, but our friendship did, and that's how I came to work here," Angie was saying as Taryn entered the room. "At least we had some pretty wedding pictures to fight over during the divorce."

Taryn cringed inside at the words. Angie loved the *marriage didn't last* line, but whenever Taryn heard it, it always made her feel as nauseated as she had been on the fishing boat. As much as she tried to convince herself that she was only responsible for the ceremonies and not the marriages, she couldn't help believing that if she made the wedding day magical and personal enough, the rest of the relationship couldn't be less than perfect.

At least today's clients didn't seem uncomfortable with the mention of divorce in their wedding planner's office, and they were laughing along with Angie in what seemed to be a genuine way.

"Ah, here's the wedding genius now," Angie said. "She'll get your plans sorted in no time."

"Thank you, Angie," Taryn said, smiling at her before turning to the tall, dark-haired man. She recognized him from the news, as well as from her research after he had called the office last week. He was the mayor of the nearby town of Sumner. Not exactly world-famous, but a well-known local figure, and one who seemed poised to move into higher political circles in the years ahead. If he ended up hiring her, he would be one of her most prestigious clients, and an influential contact to have. "You must be Martin Hannah. It's a pleasure to meet you, Mr. Mayor."

"Call me Marty," he said, with the booming voice of someone accustomed to speaking in front of crowds. "And this is my partner, Lex Adel."

"Taryn Ritter." She shook their hands and led them into her office. As usually happened, they immediately were drawn to the photos on the walls, walking in a circuitous route that took them past each picture before they arrived at the chairs she had placed by her desk.

She observed them as they gestured at the pictures and chatted about certain ones, noticing that they each seemed to have carefully cultivated a specific look. Marty was as put-together as he always looked in press shots or on the news. His high-quality slacks, button-down shirt, and cashmere sweater gave the impression that he would be appropriately dressed for any mayoral situation that arose, but the clothes were unobtrusive enough to let his larger-than-life personality shine through.

Lex, though, was more studiously casual with their tightly curled, close-cropped hair and fitted flannel shirt and jeans. They could be the cover model for an L.L.Bean catalog, while Marty looked poised to step into any boardroom and take charge of a high-powered meeting. The two were point and counterpoint—one down-to-earth and the other destined for press conferences and power lunches.

"You've done beautiful work," Lex said as they sat down, startling Taryn out of her mental observations. "And such a variety."

Taryn smiled her thanks. "No two couples are alike, so why should all weddings be the same? I love making dreams come true, no matter how nontraditional they are. So, how can I help you plan *your* perfect wedding?"

As always, she added the slight emphasis on the word *your*, implying with one word that yes, those photos were nice, but the only wedding that mattered now was the one they were about to plan together. That sentence, delivered just the right way, triggered the expressions of excitement she loved seeing on her clients' faces. For someone who prided herself on planning unique weddings, her work from start to finish on a project followed predictable and consistent patterns. The details might change, but the process stayed the same.

"We want to get married in the cat café in Sumner," Marty said.

Taryn nodded, careful not to repeat the phrase. She had learned early in her career that clients responded defensively when she did that, even if she didn't intend to sound disbelieving or critical. They seemed to hear the word *really?* even when it wasn't spoken, probably because most everyone else they had told about their idea had questioned their choices. *A cat café? Really?* Or *A turtle? Really?*

He smiled at Lex. The warmth in the glance they shared transcended the conspicuously balanced images they portrayed. They were simply two people in love, and Taryn would never stop feeling proud and honored to be invited to share in these moments with her clients. "It's where we met."

"Where we all met," Lex added with a laugh.

"All of you?" Okay she repeated that one, but she needed to know how many people were involved in this wedding if she was planning the event.

"The two of us, and our two cats," Lex clarified.

"Ah, of course." Two humans and two cats. She might have more conversations with vets in her future. "And will they be part of the ceremony?"

"Oh no," Marty said. "They wouldn't enjoy it. You know how cats are."

"Yes, I sure do," Taryn agreed. She didn't, but she'd take Marty's word for it that they didn't enjoy weddings as much as turtles did.

"We'll have a public reception at the Town Hall," he continued, "but later, after we're back from our honeymoon. We want the ceremony to be more intimate, although the local press will have to be invited. My campaign slogan called Sumner the City with Heart, and this cat café is a business with heart. This is a way for us to celebrate our relationship, and at the same time honor my role as Sumner's mayor by highlighting one of the city's most cherished locations."

Taryn glanced at Lex, but they didn't seem upset by the idea that Marty saw a political angle to their wedding. She was glad, since this constant blending of personal and public life was going to be a way of life for the two of them if Marty's career took him to state or federal offices. She would do her best to make sure this wedding incorporated as much of the personal side for both of them as possible and let Marty and the press handle the political aspects.

They spoke for a while longer, until Taryn felt their vision for the wedding start to gel in her mind. Decorations and menu choices, seating arrangements and other logistics for moving the couple and their guests comfortably through the day—

those more concrete plans would have to wait until she saw this cat café in person. Right now, she concentrated on the more ephemeral vibe of the wedding, how they wanted the event to project who they were.

She got as many details as she needed for the first stage of planning and eventually said good-bye to Marty and Lex, reminding them to ask about cat allergies when they interviewed prospective officiants. She was relieved that they hadn't bothered to ask her, as their wedding planner, that same question. She had no idea whether she was allergic to cats—or really, any animals—or not.

She searched for the café online but didn't find a website or any information beyond a listing on the Sumner Chamber of Commerce site, which at least gave her an address. She didn't know much about cat cafés beyond the fact that she was pretty sure they had cats *in* them and not on the menu. It didn't sound very sanitary, but she didn't need to eat the food.

She just needed to plan the wedding and get a cute kitty photo for her wall.

She jotted down the café's address. She had some work to do here at the office in the morning, so she'd head out to Sumner after she finished and get the details ironed out with the owner. They'd probably be thrilled to have the mayor and all his publicity take over the café for one day. She'd surely be done with that by lunch, so she continued scrolling through the Chamber of Commerce site, searching for a non-pet-related restaurant to try while she was in Marty's beloved City with a Heart.

CHAPTER THREE

B onnie's cell rang at five thirty in the morning, triggering the usual groggy panic she experienced with too-early calls. She flung herself across the bed, her mind racing through panicked scenarios of fires or robberies, and grabbed the phone, causing a small avalanche of cats as the three that had been sleeping on her legs toppled off. Her two older cats leaped off the bed in a huff, but her little striped kitten merely curled into a ball next to her and went back to sleep.

Bonnie saw her mother's name on the screen and flopped onto her pillow with a groan. Yes, someone might be dying, but more likely her mother was too excited to wait until a reasonable hour to call Bonnie and tell her about the latest pregnancy or promotion in the James family. She had four siblings and six cousins who routinely churned out either babies or ginormous pay raises, each one widening the gap between their lives and hers. She didn't want those things, but her mother seemed to think that hearing about them constantly would somehow be inspirational for her.

She briefly considered letting the call go to voice mail, but she'd only be delaying the inevitable. She swiped to answer, ending the insistent ringing. "Hi, Mom."

"Good morning, darling," her mother said in a breezy

voice, as if it wasn't still dark outside. "I hope I didn't wake you, but I couldn't wait to share the news. Jonah's getting married!"

Bonnie rubbed her eyes, trying to force her mind into a more alert state. Jonah. Her oldest brother, a stay-at-home dad with four kids and a wife who beamed her way into thousands of homes every day as one of the hosts on a top Seattle morning show. He'd been held up as an aspirational ideal for her since high school, when he had married the former Miss Washington. Bonnie didn't recall there ever being a divorce, but she probably wouldn't get a call about one of those.

"Isn't he already married?" she asked, stifling a yawn. Once the initial panic about the ringing phone had been eased, her body just wanted to go back to sleep. She climbed out of bed and scooped up Pepper, taking the kitten with her into the kitchen.

"Of course. He and Mayu are blissfully happy, of course. They're renewing their vows."

"Why?" The obvious answer was that he was doing this to make her look bad. She could imagine this tacked on to her aunt's litany of laments next time the family was together for a holiday. *Look at Jonah. He's had two weddings now, and you haven't even had one.*

"To celebrate their fifteenth wedding anniversary, of course."

"Hmm…" she said, unconvinced. She had a more cynical explanation. She loved Jonah, but he was addicted to their parents' approval. He thrived on it to the same extent that she stubbornly rejected it. She figured he needed some big event to fill the gap between the birth of their fourth child and the arrival of the first grandkid, so why not recycle the wedding furor?

She fed her cats and struggled to get dressed with her phone in her hand while her mom chatted on about bridesmaid dresses and a harpist, since apparently this was going to be another exhausting full wedding, and not just an intimate *Let's renew our vows on a beach in Barbados as an excuse for a fancy vacation* kind of thing.

She had been on the periphery of wedding planning eight times now. The only other two in this generation of her immediate family not to be married were her older sister who traveled extensively as a financial analyst for an international corporation—Bonnie had always been a bit hazy on the details, but she thought her sister was currently in the UAE—and her cousin who was a professional baseball player and had enough women available for dating not to be interested in settling down with just one of them.

Her family seemed to believe those were better reasons to not be married than having a lot of cats.

"Sounds great, Mom," she interjected eventually, breaking in on the monologue about reception halls. "I'll call Jonah later and congratulate him. Again. I should go now, though. I need to get to the café and take care of the cats."

"Oh yes. The cats." To her mother's credit, she didn't add the comment *Don't you wish they were babies instead?* She might as well have, though, because Bonnie knew it was hovering in the air, unsaid this time but too often spoken out loud.

Bonnie left her house and quickly walked the six blocks to her café. She was happy to have found a place to rent that was close enough for her to check on the cats before bed, but she would feel more comfortable once she was living on the property. She almost had enough saved to expand into the backyard, creating a dedicated room for the afternoon teas and opening up the main bedroom suite for her original plan of moving into it. Today, though, she was glad to have the walk, with time to clear her head after her mother's call and before she started her workday.

She loved her family, as frustrating as they could be sometimes. She adored her nieces and nephews and her numerous little first cousins once removed, and they always seemed excited to come visit her café where they spent hours eating cookies and playing with the cats. She was proud of her siblings' and cousins' accomplishments, and they seemed to genuinely care about her and want her to be happy and fulfilled, too.

The problem was, she didn't fit her family's idea of *fulfillment*. She had been raised in a household that measured success in terms of either large broods of children or prestigious careers—and having both was a bonus. She had chosen a life path that offered neither when she took a job with a nonprofit when she graduated college. No one in her family had known quite what to make of her.

She liked it that way. She was proud of herself for rejecting the goals she had been told since childhood that she should seek—not because they weren't wonderful things for people who wanted them, but because they were wrong for her. She had forged a path for herself on her own terms. Sure, her time in the nonprofit sector had been awkwardly cut short, but she had bounced back and opened her café. The journey had sometimes been a lonely one, but she had plenty of love in her life, human and feline.

She exhaled, letting go of the residual stress from the morning's conversation before she entered her café, and got swept up by the busyness of the day.

❖

Bonnie wiped down the counters and tossed the tea towel she was using into the basket full of linens that needed to be washed. The ovens were full of baking trays, and the lunch sandwiches were wrapped and ready to go for the afternoon. She looked around, for once rather desperate for another task to demand her attention.

Nothing. Damn.

She stepped out of the kitchen to the counter area. The café was quiet, with only two tables occupied—both by people who were reading books with cats in their laps. The breakfast rush had finished, and lunch customers would be arriving soon. Jerome had swapped his afternoon shift for Isa's morning today, and he was walking through the café, gathering scattered toys and messing with his phone.

Bonnie sighed. He hadn't been working for her long, and she loved how wonderful he was with both cats and customers, but he spent far too much time on his cell. He never failed to put it down and give patrons his full attention, but she still felt she had to say something about it. She was dreading this conversation more than nail-trim weekend.

He noticed her standing by the register and nodded at her, coming over and dumping the toys into some bins by the counter, where afternoon customers would be able to find them. "Do you mind if we sit for a minute?" he asked. He gestured at a small table along the back wall. "We need to talk."

Wasn't that her line?

"Um, sure," she said, pulling out one of the chairs. Maybe he wanted to tell her how much he loved working here, and that she was the best boss ever. If so, she'd say screw it, and let him stay on his phone as much as he wanted.

"You need a website," he said instead. "Why don't you have one yet?"

She sat down, and Sasha, a small white cat with a few scattered spots of striped gray-brown fur, leaped onto her lap and started kneading her legs, purring loudly. She looked like a tabby who was dressed as a Halloween ghost with a couple extra holes cut out of the sheet. Bonnie absently scratched behind the cat's ears as she considered the unexpected question.

"I started to make one a few weeks ago," she said, then frowned as she considered her answer. Was it months, not weeks? She remembered the trees being covered in fall-colored leaves. "Anyway, I got busy, and when I got back to it, a lot of cats had been adopted. It seemed to be too much work to keep up with how often the cat population here changes, so I just focus on getting their photos on the adoption sites."

He shook his head as if her answer was woefully inadequate. "You need to advertise the café, not just the cats. You can maybe have a page highlighting a few of them, so it's easier to update, but you also need to have the menu online, with some info about the seasonal specialties. People will come here for the cats in general and the chill atmosphere and the food, and then they'll fall in love with a specific cat. Or two or three."

Bonnie sighed. He was right, of course. This was the reason she had started building the site in the first place. She'd just need to make the time to get it done. "Okay, I'm convinced. I'll do it."

He shook his head. "No, I'll do it. It'll be my class project for my intro to web design course, just like Isa is doing your books for her business class."

"She's not doing my books. She's just using the café as a real-life example for her assignments." Unless she proved to be really good at it. Then she could do the books. And Jerome could make her website. And when the two of them graduated and left the café, she'd hire a construction student who could build her a tearoom as his class project. Or maybe an engineering student who could design a really good self-cleaning litter box.

Jerome handed her his phone, breaking her out of that particularly enticing daydream.

"Look," he said. "I've been getting tons of photos for the site, plus making notes on all the cats. I've even got some quotes from customers that we can put on the different pages."

Bonnie took the phone. The first picture was of the woman sitting across the café from them—the image was a peaceful one, with the mug of coffee and book resting on the small wooden table, and the sleepy black cat Kip curled on her lap. She scrolled through a series of photos, smiling at the way Jerome had captured the personalities of the different resident cats.

"I thought you were texting all this time," she said, relieved that she hadn't reprimanded him before he had a chance to call her out on her lack of online presence.

"At work?" he asked in an indignant voice. "Of course not. We should get at least a basic site up and running now because it might take me most of the quarter to do it right. I'll have to work in sections, so I can turn in each step as an assignment for class. But you need to have at least a home page ASAP with some pics and the café's hours to post in response to the mayor's Tweet."

Bonnie looked up from the photo of the small ginger cat Kumquat peering down from the highest post on a cat tree. "What Tweet? And what mayor?"

"Sumner's mayor—Marty Hannah. It's gone viral. Well, as viral as something in Sumner can go, which means about thirty people have Retweeted it." He took his phone back and pulled up his Twitter account before handing it back to her. "Still, lots more have written comments. I'm surprised you haven't seen it. What have you been doing all day?"

"Making chocolate croissants," Bonnie said, glancing at the screen. Playing around online was usually reserved for evenings for her, or the occasional break after the lunch crowd. "Oh, how sweet. He found love at Sumner's cat café. He did—he and his partner adopted two tuxedo cats. Tango and Rumba."

"He doesn't mean the cats," Jerome said, rolling his eyes. "He means his partner. Keep reading."

Bonnie read the post again. Marty and Lex were getting married. That was nice. She had met with the two of them several times while they were going through the adoption process and she had liked them. She hadn't realized they had met each other for the first time here, though.

She started reading through the comments and felt herself getting more tense with each one. They started with generic messages of congratulations, but sprinkled among them were comments that were more worrisome.

"*I want to meet a man who will like my three cats. Maybe I should look for him at the café,*" she read. "And this one says they thought the grocery store was the place to pick up women, but this café sounds even better. Jerome, this is awful."

He shrugged, not seeming to share her concern over the comments. "They're potential customers, and then potential adopters. The mayor just gave you a bunch of free advertising, and you should take advantage of it. Play it up."

"Play it up? No way. Let's just hope this dies out fast. This is just…"

Bonnie faded to silence, unable to articulate why this bothered her so much. Her mother might not be on Twitter, but someone in the family surely was. She could hear the comments now—*Everyone else seems to be finding love in that café of yours. Why can't you?*

She put the phone on the table. "A website is great, but I'd better not see little cupids flying around on it. The cats are what matter here. They're not just fluffy bits of decor in a trendy club."

Jerome held up his hands in a sign of surrender. "No cupids, I promise. Too bad, though." He leaned forward and lowered his voice. "Those two customers over there have been glancing at each other and smiling for the past hour. I was thinking we could have a whole page dedicated to couples that met here and the cats they adopted together."

Bonnie shook her head. "I think I liked you more when I thought you were messaging your friends or playing games than I do now that I know you're plotting to turn the café into a meat market."

He laughed. "Maybe we could have a blind date kind of event. Customers can draw the name of their date and a cat out of a hat, then have a coffee together."

Bonnie picked up Sasha and handed her to Jerome. "I'm going to put out the lunch menu," she said, walking away from his gleeful laughter.

She was going to go about her day like normal. Serving lunch—nothing heart-shaped on the menu—and taking care of cats. Hopefully, by this evening the whole fiasco would have blown over, and Sumner's online population would move on to something new.

Love was fine, and she was happy for Lex and Marty. A website focused on the cats and the baked goods was also okay. But too much attention on the café might lead to more attention on her than she was willing to accept. Spotlights tended to bring forward embarrassing shadows from the past, and Bonnie wanted nothing more than to avoid that altogether.

CHAPTER FOUR

Taryn exited off Highway 410 and drove alongside the train tracks and toward Sumner's main street, which was actually named Main Street.

It was a nice town, with both quaint and modern characteristics that made it appealing to tourists and locals alike, but even though it was only about ten minutes from her Puyallup home, Taryn rarely came here. If she turned right when she left her office, she could find a large indoor mall and nearly any chain store or restaurant she desired on Meridian Ave. Turn left, and she had her pick of one-of-a-kind shops and restaurants in downtown Puyallup. Sumner offered the same variety of establishments, just on a smaller scale.

Taryn drove past the vast yard of a farm supply store, with its piles of fencing supplies and huge watering troughs, before turning away from the river and entering Sumner's business district. She knew if she continued along this road, she'd find fast-food places and some department stores, but the first few blocks of Main Street had a carefully cultivated old-fashioned feel.

Taryn had expected the café to be something tiny, wedged among the antique stores and clothing boutiques. She was surprised to find, instead, a two-story Craftsman style home on a corner lot, which must have been the very edge of town at one point. The house was painted a soft peach color with white trim that looked ready for a touch-up, and bright yellow daffodils and small shoots of pale green hosta leaves filled the tiny gardens alongside the entrance. The effect was quite charming, helped in no small part by the woman who was bending down next to a chalkboard placard. She was wearing faded jeans and a short-sleeved sky-blue top, and her blond hair fell in a soft wave just to the line of her chin.

Taryn wrenched her attention back to the road, grateful for the quiet morning streets. She had noticed far too many details, letting her gaze linger on the woman for more moments than were safe.

She took the next side street and circled around the block before parking a few doors from the café and getting out of her SUV. She walked along the sidewalk that was lined with ornamental cherry trees, carefully stepping over the huge cracks where their roots had lifted the concrete. The culprit trees were beautiful, regardless of the damage they were doing, with their gnarled, lichen-covered trunks and velvety little leaves. Most of the pale pink blossoms were strewn on the ground, though. The blooms rarely lasted long around here, since frequent spring rain and wind tore them from their branches almost as soon as the petals opened.

This would be a perfect time of year for the wedding, with guests arriving along this fairy-tale path of flower petals, but Taryn had a feeling any season would be just as flattering to this venue. It would be a cozy, fur-filled setting in the winter, or redolent with the scent of pumpkin spice lattes in the fall. And summer would bring even more colorful flowers than just the pretty spring daffodils.

The woman in front of the café stood up as Taryn approached. She had a friendly though somewhat reserved-looking smile and pale blue eyes. Maybe leaning toward green? Taryn had a feeling they would change color depending on the woman's mood and what she was wearing. She would complement the setting no matter which season Marty and Lex chose for their wedding, adding to the charm of the café.

The house and area were beautiful, and the woman who seemed to belong there was even more so. As far as Taryn was concerned, the only real drawback to having the wedding here was the cats. She had planned plenty of weddings at zoos and farms, but then the animals were usually separated from the guests. Timmy the turtle was one of the exceptions, but he was unlikely to climb on the counters and shed fur onto the appetizers. Still, it was not her wedding. If her clients wanted a houseful of cats, they were getting them.

"Hello," Taryn said. She gestured at the sign next to the door. "Are you Bonnie?"

"Yes, I am," Bonnie said, shaking the hand Taryn offered with only a slight hesitation. She probably didn't regularly have customers approaching her in such a businesslike manner, and Taryn sensed that she needed to alter her approach slightly.

"I'm Taryn," she said, omitting her surname at the last moment since Bonnie hadn't offered hers, and to make herself seem more like a casual patron than someone who would really prefer to get this matter settled in time to find a less furry place for lunch.

She had been relieved to see the shop listed on Sumner's Chamber of Commerce site as Bonnie's Cat Café. She had been worried it would be the Kittens and Bows Tea Salon or something equally ridiculous that she would have a hard time saying without laughing. At least this name showed its owner's practical side. We're a café. We have cats. Period.

Of course, the cartoon cat and mice drawings on the chalkboard menu next to Bonnie revealed a more whimsical side. Taryn found it a bit alarming to have mice on any piece of advertising for a dining establishment. Not that this place would be likely to have a mouse problem for long, given its residents, but still…

Taryn skimmed over the rest of the menu, not really interested since she wouldn't be staying, then did a double take. "Oh, rhubarb pie. That's my favorite."

"Freshly baked this morning," Bonnie said, with a warm hint of pride in her voice. She put her hand on the doorknob. "Were you just passing by, or coming in?"

"Coming in, please," Taryn said, walking into the foyer when Bonnie opened the door for her. She waited for Bonnie to shut the outer door—several very conspicuous signs demanded she do so—and then went into the café's main room.

Taryn was momentarily distracted by the scent of baked goods—delicious—and the sight of all the cats—there really were a lot of them!—but her years of experience in this job kicked in, and she analyzed the room in moments.

How they would arrange the tables.

Where Marty and Lex would sit.

Where the aisle and altar would be best situated.

She saw the room with an overlay of the wedding as if she had a window to the future. The café would require very little in the way of decorations. The walls, containers full of toys, and comfy chairs were bright with a variety of pastel colors, eased by the beige cat trees and richly brown wooden tables. The cats were all sorts of colors, dotted here and there on beds or customer's laps. They wouldn't even need to add flowers, which was good since the cats would probably destroy them, or she'd buy the wrong kind and poison them, and neither of those outcomes would enhance the wedding.

"Did you want to order, or are you looking for someone?"

Bonnie asked, and Taryn realized she had been motionless for longer than it should take for a customer to locate the counter.

"Yes, but first I want to…oh…well…" Taryn's voice faltered to a stop as she felt a weight thump onto her foot. She looked down and found a cat stretched across her shoe, making kneading motions in the air with its paws and occasionally snagging on her black pants. The cat was white, with a few funny round patches of striped fur. Its tail was the same striped pattern, as was the jaunty little beret-shaped marking on its head. Unfortunately, only the white fur seemed to be shedding, and Taryn now had a swath of it across her hemline.

"That's Sasha," Bonnie said. "Wow, she seems quite taken with you. It's like you have a special bond."

"Really?" Taryn asked, forgetting to hide the disbelief in her voice until the word was out. Was this the usual hard sell approach to making customers adopt cats, or was she going to have to break a feline heart today? Taking the cat home was certainly not an option. She tried to subtly shift her foot, but the cat was like a dead weight on her shoe.

Bonnie laughed. "No, sorry. She loves everyone. Luckily, she has a thick skin and won't be offended by the horrified expression you had on your face when I said that. Don't worry, adoption isn't a requirement for getting a piece of pie."

Taryn tried to deny it, but she couldn't help joining in Bonnie's laughter. This playful side of her seemed at odds with the way Taryn had felt her holding herself at a slight distance during the rest of their interaction.

"I was dubious, not horrified," Taryn said, directing her comment in the cat's direction with a smile.

"Are you more of a dog person than a cat person?" Bonnie asked.

Neither was obviously not an acceptable answer. Not that

Taryn actively disliked either one—she was just neutral on the subject of all pets. They were for other people. Her present life was too busy for her to take on the responsibility of an animal, and her childhood…well, pets deserved a happy home, didn't they?

"No," she fibbed. "I love cats. They're so independent." Taryn parroted back the phrase she had heard from every cat owner she had ever met. She looked down at Sasha, who was purring so deeply Taryn could feel the vibrations of it moving up her leg. "Well, except this one."

Bonnie bent down and picked up the cat, brushing her shoulder against Taryn's thigh as she stood up again. She quickly stepped away. "But first…?" she prompted.

Taryn took a moment to regain the thread of their conversation, caught by surprise at the loss of warmth on her foot and the very different sort of heat Bonnie had inadvertently trailed across her leg.

"Oh. Yes. I actually came by because I'm a wedding planner. Martin Hannah, your mayor, and his partner Lex would love to rent your café for their wedding, so I was hoping we could sort out the details."

Bonnie's expressions had been mild so far—a little cool, a little playful—but now she closed herself off from Taryn with an unmistakable decisiveness, like a slamming door.

Taryn nearly stepped back in surprise but caught herself in time and kept her own expression neutral. She had expected Bonnie to be flattered. Proud, maybe, to be singled out by the mayor. Borderline angry, though? That hadn't even crossed Taryn's mind. Maybe she was vehemently opposed to him politically, but that didn't seem to be a likely reason for her to be reacting this way. Marty and Lex had made it sound as if they had been regular, welcome customers here.

"So you're responsible for the Tweets," Bonnie said coolly.

"What? I'm on Twitter, but only for business. Promotions, that sort of thing." She pulled her phone out of her pocket and opened the Twitter app. "What am I looking for?"

Before Bonnie had a chance to answer, Taryn figured it out. She was tagged in Marty's original post, and she scanned the responses. "He mentions the café," she said, scrolling as she tried to locate whatever comment had made Bonnie bristle. "The responses seem kind of cute. Good advertising for you, at least. Oh, the grocery store one is funny. Let me know which post offended you, and I'll take care of it."

Bonnie shook her head. "Funny? It's not funny to have people treating my café like the town's hot romance spot."

Bonnie's voice had risen slightly in pitch, and Taryn automatically lowered her own. "I hardly think that's going to happen. You might get one or two people who come here hoping to find love, but I doubt your cat café will replace online dating or clubs. Although, maybe you could pitch a new show to a TV network. Sort of like *The Bachelor*. You could call it *Brewing Love at the Cat Café*." Taryn laughed, then put her hand to her mouth to try to hide it when Bonnie's glower increased. Something about her frown seemed a bit forced now, though. It was almost too belligerent, as if Bonnie was maybe trying to hide a smile of her own behind the threatening expression.

"Sorry, sorry," Taryn said, schooling her features back to neutral. She was usually a pro at playing the role of cool and emotionless wedding planner, but something about Bonnie made her filters malfunction. "I know, it's not funny. I can talk to Marty and have him tone down the lovey-dovey stuff next time he mentions your café. Maybe he can post a correction.

Say he mistyped, and they actually fell in love at the gas station down the street."

"The smell of gasoline will give the wedding a nice cosmopolitan touch," Bonnie said, setting Sasha down and crossing her arms over her chest. "Please tell Marty and Lex I'm sorry, but we can't accommodate a wedding here. I'll be sure to give them a free celebratory coffee and pastry next time they stop by."

"Okay," Taryn said, abruptly switching tactics. Bonnie raised her eyebrows, obviously surprised that Taryn was giving up so easily.

Of course, Taryn wasn't giving up at all, just redirecting. One lesson she had learned very well was that a yes was lurking behind every no. She just had to regroup and figure out how to access the response she wanted.

"I know a lost cause when I see one. I'll just have some of your rhubarb pie and a…" She glanced at the main drink menu on the wall behind the counter and finished her order with only the tiniest hesitation. "And a meow-cha, please."

"Fine. Have a seat, and we'll bring it out to you. Did you want to sit in our new singles section, or do you see another customer you like? I'll be happy to make the introductions."

Taryn had a keen sense of precisely how far most people's personal-space bubbles extended, and she deliberately stepped just inside of Bonnie's. "Well, you're kind of cute. Care to join me?"

Bonnie huffed, not moving away from Taryn. "Given that my reason for declining this wedding is because I don't want you turning my café into Tinder With Cats, I hardly think that flirting with me is the way to get what you want."

Unless Bonnie was what she wanted, which she most definitely was *not*. She just managed to bring out those parts of Taryn she usually had an easy time repressing. Taryn eased back. "What can I say? I can't resist a challenge. I'll do my best to recover from your rejection and just pick a random seat. Let destiny work its magic."

"Good luck with that," Bonnie said, turning away and heading over to the counter.

Taryn picked a table along the back wall, far from the other two customers, and Sasha hopped onto her lap the moment she sat down. Taryn looked up to see Bonnie watching her with raised eyebrows, as if daring Taryn to evict the cat. Taryn just shrugged, not taking the bait. Aside from it being a point of pride not to let Bonnie know she wasn't completely comfortable around animals, Sasha was a tiny little thing, barely a significant weight on her lap. She'd be practically unnoticeable if not for her warm body and unexpectedly throaty purr. Taryn would be cleaning white fur off these pants later anyway, so what was a little more?

Besides, far more disturbing than little Sasha was the large orange cat perched on a carpet-covered ledge on the far wall that was staring at her as if he was a tiger and she the baby wildebeest in a nature documentary.

She looked away from the cat when the young man who had been working the espresso machine brought her a plate with a generous wedge of pie and a drink with a smiling cat head stenciled on the foam in cocoa powder. After she thanked him, she glanced back to where the cat had been, but now it was on the ground and a few feet closer to her, still sitting in the same half-crouched pose as if it had materialized in the new position.

She scooped up a forkful of pie and ate it, mostly forgetting about Ninja Cat as her taste buds exploded with flavors that epitomized spring in the Northwest. Tart, cinnamony rhubarb chunks melted in her mouth, balanced by the buttery, flaky pastry with its interesting layer of sugary crunch. If the orange cat killed her now, she'd die happy and fulfilled.

And if Bonnie was the one who had made this pie, Taryn was going to insist that she do the catering for the wedding, which she had no doubt *would* take place here. Bonnie might not want her café to be known as a place to find romance, but Taryn *did* want to be known as the wedding planner who could work miracles.

And when it came to a contest of stubbornness and determination, she'd back herself every time.

CHAPTER FIVE

And she actually expected me to say yes!" Bonnie continued, recounting her meeting with that wedding planner to her friend Viv Meriwether at brunch the following Sunday.

Taryn Ritter.

Not that Bonnie had dug Taryn's business card out of the fishbowl on the counter to find out her last name. It had been right on top, where Taryn had put it when she came to the register to pay, and it had been easily readable through the glass with only a minor bit of shaking needed to flip it faceup. Not that Bonnie cared what her name was. She had merely wanted to know so she'd be prepared if Taryn won the monthly drawing for a free Kittens and Cream Tea. She'd manage to be out sick that day.

"Well, thank goodness you said no," Viv said, calmly pouring warmed syrup over her waffles. "Just think of all the new customers the publicity would bring in. Whatever would you do with all that extra money?"

"Exactly. Publicity," Bonnie said, glossing over the money and new customers parts of Viv's comment. "Everything the mayor does is made public. She didn't bring it up, but I'll bet the photos would be in the paper. Or," she added, horrified at the thought, "they might even expect the press to be at the wedding."

"Shocking," Viv said mildly, sipping at her mimosa. "You sure dodged a bullet there."

"I sense sarcasm," Bonnie said, smiling at Viv in spite of her lingering indignation at Taryn's request.

She used her index finger to wipe the edge of her overflowing plate of biscuits and gravy, sighing with pleasure as she licked it clean. Sundays were Bonnie's day off—although *day off* was a relative phrase in her world—and she and Viv had brunch together at least once a month. They always vowed that the next month they would try someplace new and exciting, and they always ended up returning to Sumner's Southern Kitchen. The food was never disappointing, although today Bonnie did have some complaints about Viv's lack of commiseration.

"I don't think you fully appreciate what a..." Bonnie frowned as she tried to find the right word. Violation came to mind, but even she had to admit it was far too strong for this situation. "What an intrusion this would be. For the cats."

"Pfft," Viv scoffed, waving away Bonnie's words. "Those cats of yours love people. They won't be able to tell the difference between regular customers and wedding guests."

"Well, then, it will be an intrusion for me."

Bonnie chewed a bite of food while she tried to find words to explain her feelings. She needed to have her arguments against this wedding clear in her mind for when Taryn returned. Because even though Taryn had pretended to accept Bonnie's refusal, Bonnie had no doubt Taryn would eventually return.

Bonnie hadn't been able to pin down Taryn very easily. She had been, at turns, composed and playful and flirtatious. Every time Bonnie thought she had her figured out, Taryn slipped out of one pigeonhole and into another. That was just during the few minutes in which they'd interacted—what would an hour or a day with her be like? Or a night?

Bonnie coughed and took a drink of her water, forcing her thoughts back on track. She didn't manage it quickly enough to escape Viv's notice.

"So, tell me more about this Taryn," she said, grinning as she speared a strawberry and pointed it in Bonnie's direction. "You keep going a little pink around the edges when you talk about her, and I'm guessing you were just now thinking about her because it happened again."

"I'm turning pink from annoyance," Bonnie said. "She was fine. Not *fine*-fine, so stop laughing. Just normal fine."

With dark chestnut hair that brushed the tops of her ears—delicately curved ears that Bonnie had only imagined licking for one teeny, practically nonexistent second. Taryn had been fully clothed in attire appropriate for the boardroom, but her black pants had been fitted enough to show the shape of her hips and legs. And when Bonnie's shoulder had brushed against her thigh—

"It's happening again," Viv said dryly.

Bonnie kept her observations of Taryn to herself and instead said the most damning phrase possible—not damning to Taryn as a person, of course, but the most potent argument against Bonnie ever even considering having a relationship with her.

"She's not a cat person."

Taryn had pretended she was, but Bonnie hadn't been fooled. She hadn't been mean at all and hadn't seemed to actively dislike the cats, but she had carried herself with a held-breath sort of stillness whenever Sasha had come near.

"So just have sex with her. Then you never have to see her again once the wedding is over."

"No wedding," Bonnie said with a shake of her head, more

to dislodge the word *sex* from her mind than to emphasize her denial. She knew she'd move from a little pink to full-blown neon red if she let the conversation move in that direction. While it was a detour she might be willing to take—mentally, at least—on her own, it wasn't something she cared to discuss at brunch. "It would completely ruin the image of the café if people only saw it as some sort of matchmaking center."

"I think you're deflecting," Viv said, luckily allowing Bonnie to steer the focus away from Taryn and sex. "I'm betting it wouldn't bother you if someone came to the café only because they heard you make the best cinnamon chip scones in the world, and then they spent a pleasant afternoon eating their scone and visiting with some cats. So why is this any different?"

"That is a perfectly reasonable argument," Bonnie admitted after a slight hesitation. "But I am not feeling perfectly reasonable right now. Yes, I might be overreacting just a smidge, but I spent my life trying to get away from the expectations everyone had of me getting married and having a house full of babies. I live the way I do because I rejected those traditional expectations, and I don't want them becoming permanently part of my café's image."

"This isn't exactly a conventional marriage they're proposing. It's a ceremony for two people who found their own kind of love, not the kind that society has told them they should have. There's nothing wrong with wanting that in their lives. Just because you don't date—"

"I date all the time," Bonnie said indignantly, gesturing at the room around them.

"You do? Why haven't I…Wait. Are you calling this a date?"

"Yes," Bonnie said. She had found her own kind of love,

like Viv was just saying about Marty and Lex. "Of course I am."

"You do realize I'm straight, don't you? And married?"

Bonnie rolled her eyes. "Again, yes. I was your maid of honor, remember? Which is further proof that I'm not opposed to weddings and love in general."

"So how is this a date?"

"How is it not one? We intentionally set aside time to spend together, making this a priority over anything else we could have been doing right now. We arranged when to meet and where, and we are enjoying each other's company. Relationships don't need a romantic element to give them meaning, do they?"

"Well, obviously not, but I'm talking about romantic dating, with expectations for the future."

Bonnie shrugged and sopped up the last of her gravy with a bite of biscuit. "I expect we'll have brunch together again next month."

Viv finished her mimosa and reached for Bonnie's half-empty one. "You're deliberately misdirecting this conversation. You know what a real date is, and I don't think you've been on one since you opened your café."

Bonnie sighed, momentarily letting go of her need to avoid any mention of her past. "You don't understand what a pain it is to date after...well, since I left my old job. People google you before the date, and then I'd have to spend the entire evening either trying to explain what they found or listening to stupid jokes about it. First dates are awkward enough without bringing the past into them."

Viv shook her head with a frown. "I get that, Bonnie, but don't you think it's time to start again? The internet has a short memory, and what was viral a few years ago might as well have happened in prehistoric times. It might be safe to put yourself out there again because—no offense—you're old news."

"Right," Bonnie said, circling back to her attempts to explain to Viv why she was against having Marty and Lex get married at her café. "And I'll do whatever it takes to keep it that way. Inviting the press into my café for this wedding is just asking for trouble."

"I didn't mean you were misdirecting that part of the conversation," Viv said, waving Bonnie's now empty glass at her. "I'm bored with that. Besides, it's obvious you're going to say yes to this Taryn person eventually. You'll give in because the café means too much to you, and because you're too nice to ruin their wedding plans because of your own hang-ups. What I want to know is whether you plan on spending the rest of your life *dating* only your married friends. If it's because you don't have romantic feelings for anyone, then I'll support you one hundred percent, you know that. But if it's because you don't feel you deserve to find love, or that you're not worth being loved, or because you can't let go of the past, then get ready for the longest, sternest lecture of your life."

Bonnie smiled. Her friend's sentiments were heart-warming, even though the glare Viv was currently giving her was a little frightening. And her assertion that Bonnie was going to cave to Taryn's request was ludicrous.

Hopefully.

Bonnie chose to let that comment of Viv's slide and focus instead on the rest of her little speech. "Neither one. Look Viv, dating just isn't a priority in my life right now. I spend my days baking in the kitchen and surrounded by cats. Who would want to marry into that?"

Viv tapped her chin thoughtfully. "Well, granted you'll probably have to remove the gluten intolerant people who are allergic to cats from your potential dating pool, but you'd still have a reasonably large population available that could date you without sneezing or suffering severe gastrointestinal symptoms. And if you switch to a gluten-free menu and they take antihistamines, then you have even more candidates to choose from."

Bonnie laughed. "I'll have the weirdest dating profile ever."

"Or you could just follow Marty's example and look around your café for a date. If you see any customer constantly blowing their nose or clutching their stomach, swipe left and move to the next."

❖

Later that night, Bonnie walked from her house to the café. The evening was cool but mild, after the past couple weeks of heavy wind and rain. A bright quarter moon hung low in the sky, and the streets were nearly empty. This part of Sumner closed down early, especially on the weekends, and most of the cars passing by were heading toward or away from the fast-food restaurants and bars on the other end of town.

She had spent a relaxing Sunday morning laughing with Viv over a second round of mimosas, joking about getting a commission from local allergists if she promised to send all her dates their way. Then she had run some errands, come back to the café to feed dinner, and headed home to feed herself and her own cats. After an evening reading with them snuggled alongside her, she had come back here for the night check.

Even on her days off, the café and its occupants shaped her routine. She was happy with the cycle of her days, but she didn't share Viv's faith that anyone except for the most devoted of cat lovers would ever consider joining such a life.

Bonnie unlocked the door to the café and walked quietly inside, calling out a soft hello to the cats. A few of them came to greet her, but most merely gave her sleepy looks and wide yawns as she walked past. They had been fed earlier and knew the routine well enough to be certain she wasn't going to do more than fill their bowls with kibble and water. She counted cats and made sure each one seemed healthy and uninjured before settling on a blanket near one of the cat beds where Sasha and the big orange cat Nancy had brought earlier this week were sleeping tangled together.

The ginger cat pretty much ignored customers and the other animals, but he and Sasha stuck close together when the café was closed. When it was open, he merely watched her interact with people from a distance. Bonnie had tried putting him in the quiet room at night, thinking he'd prefer being with other loners, but he had yowled at the door until she let him out again.

Come to think of it, the closest she had ever seen him come to another human was when Taryn had been in the café. Taryn had looked somewhat concerned as he'd edged closer to her—understandably so, since his expression could be fierce. Bonnie could have assured her that he was only wanting to get closer to Sasha and was much gentler than his hungry-lion stare implied, but she had kept her silence. She didn't mind if Taryn believed her café was full of feral creatures.

Maybe then she'd convince Marty to get married somewhere else.

Bonnie sighed. She wasn't sure what she'd say the next time Taryn came to ask about having the wedding here. Bonnie's arguments against it were weak, even in her own mind, but logic didn't change the resistance coiled deep within her. The wedding, the café's new image. Taryn herself. Everything felt dangerous to Bonnie, as if changes were coming that she wasn't prepared to handle.

Viv might believe it was safe for her to let go of her past, but she wasn't wholly convinced. The pain and embarrassment still felt too raw sometimes, and even when they receded into the background, the self-protective habits she had cemented into place seemed too hard to budge.

She got up and went into the kitchen, then switched on the oven and gathered some ingredients from the fridge. She saw a flash of movement out of the corner of her eye and looked over to see that Kip had sneaked through the door with her. He leaped onto the far counter and started washing his face with his paw. She really should put him out of the kitchen, but she let him stay while she mixed up a batch of cranberry orange muffins. She'd sanitize that counter later, and the floors were mopped every morning and night. Right now, she was just glad to have his company as she baked.

She did prep work the day before, making pie crusts and some doughs ahead of time, but she usually preferred to do her main baking on the day the items would be served, giving them the fresh from the oven taste she thought her customers deserved. When she was feeling troubled, though, she often turned to baking to help clear her mind. She'd take these muffins home and freeze them, thawing them out for her own breakfasts over the next week.

She spooned the batter into a muffin tin, letting her mind roam over the topics of weddings and Taryn and her conversation with Viv as she worked. Kip finished his grooming session and curled into a loaf shape on the counter, watching her with unblinking green eyes, his black fur glimmering under the harsh kitchen lights.

Bonnie mulled over the topic of love from all different

angles while the muffins baked and she cleaned up her mess, but she didn't come to any clear conclusions about how to handle this current situation. She decided that, most of all, she just wanted it to go away, to leave her alone in her familiar world where she was happy and didn't need to confront the idea that anything might be lacking in her life.

When she was done, she shut off the oven and carried Kip back into the main room, carefully locking the kitchen door behind her. She sat with the cats awhile longer, eating a warm, tangy muffin and letting the sound of gentle purrs work their magic on her troubled mind. Eventually, she said good-bye and closed the café, heading home over sidewalks covered with pink petals that glowed almost silver in the moonlight.

CHAPTER SIX

B y the time Angie arrived at the office on Monday morning, Taryn had already spent several hours researching cats online.

She had discovered that the internet offered an inexhaustible supply of cat-related videos, blogs, memes, and merchandise.

She had watched videos of cats doing funny things, cats befriending dogs, and cats doing nothing at all.

She had skimmed over dozens of blogs that claimed to identify the best food or litter or whatever else an owner might need to purchase. None of them agreed with each other, which seemed to her to be yet another reason why she didn't want a pet. How could she possibly figure out what to feed an animal when one site proclaimed a certain brand was the best option on the market, while another pretty much said she would be a horrible owner who should curl up in a guilt-ridden fetal position if she even considered putting that food in her cat's bowl?

She had even found videos made for cats to watch, with brightly colored birds and the occasional squirrel hopping onto a stump to eat some seeds. It was, by far, the most ridiculous thing she had ever heard of, and she vowed to herself never to reveal to *anyone* how long she sat there, mesmerized by the flickering movements of the birds and waiting for the pretty blue and yellow one to come back on screen.

"Hard at work, I see," Angie said, setting a cup of green tea next to Taryn and peering over her shoulder at the screen.

Taryn startled at the sound of her voice, resisting the irrational urge to snap her laptop shut, as if she had been caught watching porn and not a video of a rescuer bottle-feeding some tiny, orphaned kittens.

"Are you crying?"

"No, I'm not," Taryn said indignantly, closing her browser and moving the computer to one side in the slow and casual way of someone who was not embarrassed in the least by what she had been watching. "Maybe just a little misty-eyed because *I* am not made of stone."

Angie shrugged and took a sip of her coffee. "You do a good impression of it sometimes. So, I take it the trip to the cat café was a success?"

"Not exactly," Taryn admitted. She didn't feel disheartened by her temporary failure, though. She hadn't been lying when she'd told Bonnie she loved a challenge. And Bonnie seemed to be a very worthwhile challenge to take on.

Or her café, at least.

For Taryn's clients and their wedding dreams. Not for Bonnie herself.

Taryn exhaled slowly, focusing her thoughts on her job and off any foolish daydreams Bonnie might have inspired in her. Her only reason to be interested in Bonnie was because she needed to understand her in order to get her on board with Marty and Lex's plans. "Not yet, at least."

Her hours of internet meandering might have seemed like a waste of time on the surface, but at least she had come away from her session with a much better idea of what *not* to do the next time she talked to Bonnie about hosting the wedding at her café. She had been planning to use income and publicity as her top arguments when she revisited the subject with her reluctant café owner. She knew Sumner's property tax rate, and she had made a reasonable estimate of the costs of owning the house and running the café. Even a generous guess as to Bonnie's earnings wouldn't give her enough of a profit margin for her to easily turn down the lucrative potential from a special event like this one. The single day would likely make her more money than a month of normal business, especially when the amount they would pay her for catering was added to the total.

Publicity had been the second weapon in Taryn's arsenal. Pictures of the wedding and the café would spread through this small community and the surrounding areas. While this wouldn't even be a blip on the nation's screen of celebrity events, it would be a big deal in Pierce County, and for Bonnie, those would be the people who mattered. Local people who would see her café and the cats in the papers and would become customers.

Those two points were highly logical ones to make to any highly logical small business owner. Money and publicity? Yes, please. Sign me up. But Taryn was beginning to understand that—in this part of her life, at least—Bonnie was not a highly logical person.

She was a Cat Person.

Was Angie? Taryn realized she had never asked much about her assistant's personal life. Partly because she tended to hyperfocus on whatever her current job happened to be and didn't have much time to spare for small talk. Mostly, though, she was always worried that any question about Angie's life outside the office would lead to a conversation about her divorce. Which would lead to Taryn internally struggling with her unreasonable—but all too present—guilt about having failed Angie somehow. The weddings she planned were meant to be like cement, permanently linking her couples together.

"Do you have cats?" she asked, breaking past her reluctance to discuss personal topics because she believed the cat café was a personal mission for Bonnie, and not—at least not foremost—a professional one. If Taryn was going to convince her, it was going to have to come from a touchy-feely kind of place, which didn't make Taryn comfortable at all.

"Just one," Angie said, her face creasing into the sort of goofy grin Taryn had come to recognize when people talked about their cats. "Big old stray, she is. I was coming home one day with my arms full of grocery bags, and she just sauntered in when I had the door propped open. Made herself at home on my great-grandmother's chair and hasn't left the house since. They pick their owners, yes they do. Great honor to be chosen by a cat."

Angie pulled up her sleeve, revealing four parallel red welts on her forearm. "Got these just this morning when I caught her nibbling at my breakfast and tried to move her off the table." She paused and sighed. "I don't know what I would have done without her while I was going through the divorce."

Taryn rubbed her temple. She had known the divorce would come up at some point. Still, the short marriage must have been pretty awful if being routinely clawed by a cat was the preferred option. Angie's seamless leaps from dismemberment attempts to pure love were perplexing to Taryn.

"The owner of the cat café—Bonnie—said she doesn't want to have the wedding there," she said, moving the talk back to work. "And I don't think that a big rental check or the prestige of having the mayor publicizing the event are going to convince her otherwise. I've been researching animal rescuers, trying to get a better feel of how to talk to her. One thing they seem to have in common is how money and recognition seem to mean so little to them. I think if I promised Bonnie I would find one of her cats the most perfect adopted home, she might be more inclined to say yes than if I offered her double what the venue is worth. Say, do you want another cat?"

"No, I couldn't," Angie said, holding her hands up in a fending-her-off gesture, as if Taryn had a cat hidden under her desk and was about to foist it on her. "My Layla doesn't like other cats. She near tore my blinds down once, trying to get at one that was in the garden outside the window. What about you? I think a cat would suit you well. They're so independent."

"That's what everyone says about them, but the ones I met at the café don't fit that description. One had definite codependent tendencies, and the other looked homicidal." Taryn was beginning to suspect that cats were furry little aliens, practicing their mind control on the people foolish enough to get close to them.

She wasn't about to take that chance. Just one trip to the café had already snared her somehow. She still hadn't managed to get Sasha's white fur out of the weave of her favorite black pants, or the picture of Bonnie framed in the doorway of her café out of her mind. Bonnie was beautiful, in her slightly held-back way, as if there was so much more to her than most people would ever see or appreciate...

"You know," Angie continued, fortunately recapturing Taryn's wandering thoughts. "It seems you have a lot in common with this café owner...What did you say her name was?"

"Bonnie."

Angie smiled. "Bonnie. You said that in a real dreamy way. Maybe you can convince her in another way? A little wine, a nice dinner..."

"I am not going to flirt with her just to get her to sign the rental contract," Taryn said in what she hoped was a sharp, reprimanding sort of tone. "That's very unprofessional. Besides," she admitted after a slight pause, "I already tried, and she told me it wasn't going to work."

Angie laughed so hard she nearly spilled her coffee. "She's not supposed to notice what you're up to when you flirt, you know. But then subtlety's never been your strong suit, has it."

"I did just fine, thank you," Taryn lied. "She just happened to be more interested in complaining about how everyone in town is talking about her café than in appreciating the woman standing in front of her."

"Hmm. Well, give it another try, dear. You're probably just a bit rusty."

Taryn pinched the bridge of her nose. This was way too far off track—and way too close to where her thoughts had been since her meeting with Bonnie.

"Even one try was one too many. It's not as if we have anything in common, anyway. We seem about as different as two people could get."

"Yes, one of you has cats and the other doesn't. Might as well be from different species." Angie gave Taryn one of her usual supremely insubordinate eye rolls. "What I was going to say before you steered the conversation to your failed attempts to date Bonnie is that *you* could make quite a lot more money if you were a regular wedding planner, just like she could make more if she had a different job, or if she had a café that didn't include a pack of animals needing food and vet care and time. You run this business your way because you want to give your full attention to your clients. Make them feel heard and special. Just like she takes on these lonely and abandoned cats and wants nothing more than to give each of them a great life in a forever home."

Taryn frowned. She had been about to protest that she hadn't been the one to sidetrack them onto the subject of dating, and that it was more accurate to say she hadn't really tried hard to flirt with Bonnie—it had just been a playful comment, so in no way did it count as a failure.

Angie had steamrolled past the point where Taryn could interject these things, though, and what she had said next was accurate and insightful enough to catch Taryn by surprise. Her wedding planning business was a success by any standard, but she could easily double or triple her income by switching to a more conventional path in her chosen career. Planning cookie-cutter weddings would require less work on her part. Once she had the basic template and connections with a few select vendors, she would simply need to tweak the package a little to fit each new set of clients. She could juggle multiple weddings at once, while with her current approach, she rarely had more than three events in play at any one time. Less effort, more income.

Was she tempted to change? Not even a little bit.

Even when she planned weddings that were a bit more predictable or familiar to her than her clients realized, she was always able to identify and emphasize the small details that made each one unique. Couples came to her because they wanted to feel like individuals, and she took the time to treat them as such. If she had twenty events going on at the same time, or if she was always trying to gently—or not so gently—nudge her customers toward the preferred vendors who gave her the best commissions, then she wouldn't have the time or energy to spend on the phone with turtle experts or online watching birds eating seeds—neither of which would probably be of much interest to conventional, high-volume wedding planners, but both of which helped her create truly unique and meaningful days in her clients' lives.

Maybe, in this one instance of idealism, she and Bonnie might have more in common than Taryn would ever have expected. In any given month, Bonnie would probably be more thrilled to have placed a single cat in the most perfect, loving home than to have increased her profit margin or served a record number of customers. Just like Taryn would rather secure a single invitation for a turtle to attend a small, modestly budgeted wedding than to have planned six traditional events that had been lifted directly off the latest fashionable Pinterest board.

But just because she and Bonnie might share a similar sense of focus on meaning over money didn't necessarily make them compatible in any other sense.

Bonnie was attractive, yes, but Taryn was only stepping into her café and her life for a short time because she had a job to do there. Neither was a place where Taryn would want to spend much time in normal circumstances.

She was working hard to convince herself of that last thought when she realized Angie had been silent for several minutes. It was one of the gifts that made her an invaluable employee despite the fact that she was a constant reminder to Taryn of yet another failed marriage. She would often give Taryn a nudge in a new direction or say something to tweak her perspective on a subject, and then she would remain uncharacteristically quiet while Taryn mulled over what she had said.

When Taryn's focus shifted out of her internal musings, Angie gave her a smug smile. "There now. You know what matters to her, and that's what you need to offer in exchange for the café. Who knows, maybe you'll get a second chance to use those flirting skills you've been keeping on the shelf for so long." She shook her head, her smile lessening somewhat. "Might need a third and fourth chance, too, to get back on form. Let's hope this Bonnie of yours is a patient one."

Chapter Seven

Taryn left her office and arrived at the cat café near the same time she had the week before, assuming the time between morning coffee and lunch would be quiet again today. For Bonnie's sake, she hoped it was a brief lull, and not the standard for the entire day.

Today, there were three customers, with two sitting together at a table near the window and another alone by one of the tall cat trees. The woman who was by herself had an open laptop on the table in front of her and Sasha in her lap.

Huh.

Not that Taryn cared if the little white cat had transferred her affections to someone else. Someone who probably didn't care about getting cat hair all over their nice clothes, and who would adopt her and take her home. That was just great. She looked up and saw the big orange cat sitting on the highest of the stepped, carpeted ledges built into the wall. That one, at least, hadn't lost interest in her and was staring at her as if calculating the most efficient way to go for her jugular.

In what might prove to be the last move she ever made, Taryn turned her back on Ninja Cat and walked up to the register. A different person was working at the counter than on her previous visit, this one a young woman with her dark hair tied in a ponytail and a tag on her shirt with the name *Isa* surrounded by frolicking cartoon cats. She was sliding a tray of what smelled like freshly baked chocolate chip cookies into the glass-fronted cabinet, and she smiled when she looked up and saw Taryn.

"Good morning. What can I get for you?"

Taryn checked out the handwritten menu on the wall. She had appreciated the practical, straightforward name of the café, but Bonnie's quirkier side was on full display here.

"Ameri-cat-no," she said. "That's an Americano, right? Then what's a Happy Ameri-cat-no?"

Isa grinned. "An Americano with cream, of course."

"Oh. Um, cute. I'll have one of those, please."

Isa was quiet for a moment, and she looked like she was waging an internal struggle with herself. Judging by her sigh, she lost the battle. "Bonnie says I'm not supposed to serve those unless I tell you that although the image of a cat happily drinking a bowl of cream is a charming one, dairy products really aren't good for them and shouldn't be part of a healthy feline diet."

She spoke robotically, probably repeating word-for-word what Bonnie had insisted she say. Isa might think the caveat diminished the whimsy of the drink's name, but it made Taryn smile. She and Angie had been correct about what mattered to Bonnie, and it certainly wasn't the quest for profits no matter what the cost.

"I promise not to share my coffee with any of the cats," Taryn said. She wandered over to examine the baked goods while Isa brewed her drink. Some trays of Danishes and muffins looked sparse—most likely decimated by the morning customers—while the more dessert-like offerings of pies and cookies appeared to have been recently added to the case, ready for the lunch crowd.

Taryn took her mug and a plate with a strawberry muffin over to the far table where she had sat on her last visit.

Great. She had a usual table at a cat café.

There was a concept she never would have applied to herself before Marty Hannah had come into her life.

She took a bite of the streusel-covered muffin and jumped a little when she looked up and saw the orange cat had stealthily moved two shelves closer to her.

"Don't worry. He won't kill you unless I tell him to."

Taryn turned to find Bonnie standing behind her. She was wearing a green shirt today, turning her eyes the teal green of still, deep waters.

"You're back," she said.

"I'm back," Taryn agreed. "But just for some caffeine and to soak in the furry ambience. Not to argue with you about the wedding or hit on you."

"Well, that's a relief," Bonnie said, clearly not convinced. "I'll leave you to it, then."

"Wait," Taryn said, reaching out and putting her hand on Bonnie's arm to stop her. "Will you join me for a few minutes?"

Bonnie raised her eyebrows, glancing at Taryn's hand, which was still resting on her forearm. "Which one is it, then? Of those two things you just said you weren't here to do?"

Taryn laughed and let go of Bonnie. She was ultimately here about the wedding, but she had been hoping to approach the subject obliquely. After feeling the warmth of Bonnie's skin against her own, however, she was tempted to take Angie's advice and give flirting another try. She shook her head, as much to dispel the temptation as to answer Bonnie's question.

"Neither one. Really. Our talk the other day gave me an idea, and I wanted to share it with you. It's about cats."

"Oh, I've got to hear this," Bonnie muttered as she pulled out the chair and sat across from Taryn. She leaned back and crossed her arms in what was the most obvious display of closed-off body language Taryn had ever seen. And Angie said *Taryn* wasn't subtle.

"I saw the sign out front," Taryn said, toying with the handle of her mug. "You've adopted out three hundred thirty-seven cats? That's impressive for only being in business for a couple of years."

"Thank you," Bonnie said, softening a little. "We're proud of it."

Baby steps, Taryn thought. "How many cats do you usually have here at a time?"

Bonnie frowned slightly, probably trying to figure out where Taryn was going with her questions. "It varies. Right now we have twenty-four. Six are kittens, and the rest are adult cats."

"Twenty-four," Taryn repeated before she could stop herself. The number surprised her because it was higher than she had been estimating based on the cats she had seen. "And the Department of Health is okay with this?"

Taryn knew before she finished the question that it was the wrong thing to say, but for some reason her normal reticence and carefully framed sentences flew out the window when she was with Bonnie.

"I assure you, we have all the permits required for both a café and an animal rescue group. I can show you our licenses if you have any doubts."

Taryn held out her hands in a calming gesture. "I'm not a health inspector. I was just asking. I mean, it really does seem like a lot of animals to have around food."

"The cats aren't allowed in the kitchen where we prepare the food," Bonnie said. She squinted slightly and glanced over Taryn's shoulder toward the counter and the door behind it, which presumably led to the kitchen. She looked slightly concerned, as if there might in fact be a cat or two lounging on the counters as they spoke. "As for the dining area, it's not much different from eating at home with pets."

"Yeah, but who has two dozen pets at home?" Taryn asked with a laugh. Bonnie didn't seem amused, so Taryn pursed her lips and tried to assume a more serious expression. "Look, I'm not here to criticize or to challenge the legality of your business. I've eaten here twice now, so I'm obviously not concerned about how sanitary the kitchen is. I was just curious. This cat café thing is a new concept for me."

"Fine," Bonnie said, still sounding a little prickly. "Can you get to the point you were going to make?"

"Yes, of course." Taryn took a sip of her coffee and set the mug back on the table, giving herself a moment to regain her composure and focus. The attempt was foiled somewhat by the little squeak of surprise she made when Sasha suddenly jumped onto her lap and curled into a tight ball, immediately falling asleep.

Taryn smiled slightly. Ha. Take that, Laptop Woman. She glanced over and saw the customer packing her bag and getting ready to leave. Well, at least she was Sasha's second choice. Okay, really her only other option in the nearly empty café, but still, Taryn's lap had beat out a bunch of fluffy cat beds.

"So, I know you aren't interested in having a wedding here, or turning the café into a matchmaking service, but I had an idea about a way you could promote cat adoption by using the concept of speed dating. Not for people to find human partners, but to give them a chance to meet a bunch of cats."

Bonnie started to rise. "I really should get back to lunch prep—"

"Just hear me out. Please," Taryn said. Bonnie nodded

shortly and settled back in her chair. Taryn continued, speaking faster since she knew she had limited time before Bonnie walked away.

"In some ways, adopting an animal is similar to dating. You have to get past appearances and really understand what the other person or the cat is like, to know if you'd be compatible, right? Not just pick a pet because it's cute or you like its color. Well, I was thinking you could have an event where you have the cats in different rooms based on personality or special needs, and people pay to come spend time with them. Maybe a room with older, quiet cats, and one for more active ones. One for kittens, or cats that need a lot of attention. The participants would start in one room and learn about the cats there, then after a certain amount of time, they'd move to the next and a new group would take their place. You could serve a different appetizer or dessert in each room, like a progressive dinner. Not only would the participants get to spend time with a lot of different cats, but they'd be educated about their unique needs and the lifestyles they'd suit."

Bonnie was silent for a moment, and Taryn couldn't read her expression. She was either going to be thrown out and banned for life from the cat café, or she'd be moving one step closer to getting the café booked for the wedding.

"Maybe a room for bonded pairs, too," Bonnie said. "Some cats are too close to separate, which can make it harder to find them homes since we have to wait until we find someone who will take both."

"Yes," Taryn said. She fought to keep her smile under control, making it merely a friendly one and not too celebratory. "That's a great idea."

Bonnie shook her head. "It's a clever idea, but not really practical for the café. We don't have the space, for one thing—"

"You wouldn't have it here," Taryn interrupted. "If you rented a larger place for the event, you could have space for more cats. I'm sure you know plenty of other rescuers who would love to be part of this. Instead of twenty-four cats and maybe fifty people, you could have hundreds of both. A charity event like this would draw a crowd. And just think how many cats would find new homes."

Somewhere during Taryn's talk, Bonnie had uncoiled from her defensive position and now rested back in her seat with a weary looking curve in her back. Taryn was irrationally tempted to stand behind her and knead some of the visible stress from her shoulders.

Luckily, Sasha was pinning her down and keeping her from trying to touch Bonnie again.

"It's a nice thought, but even less practical than having it here," Bonnie said. "The cost, the time it would take to organize. I just don't have enough of either to spare."

"I do," Taryn said quietly. "I organize events for a living. I have connections that would help us get all the supplies at a discount. I also have an in with the mayor of Sumner, who would probably be thrilled to help us find a nice big place to rent that would be close to the café so the cats wouldn't have to be transported far. The admission fees would more than cover the basic costs, and the rest of the profits would be split among the rescue groups involved."

Bonnie stared at her for a long moment, her face expressionless. "And your fee?"

"Oh, I think you know my fee," Taryn said with a grin.

Bonnie shook her head with a rueful laugh. "You're offering me a chance to not only find homes for possibly dozens of cats, but to also educate the public about what it means to choose an animal to adopt, while at the same time helping out my friends who have their own rescue groups. And you think that's enough to get me to agree to have the wedding here?"

"Oh, I think it's more than enough," Taryn said, popping the last bite of her strawberry muffin into her mouth. It was sweet and delicious, but victory tasted even sweeter.

Bonnie crossed her arms over her chest again, but this time it seemed to Taryn to be more a gesture of semi-gracious defeat than anger. "I should say no just for spite, but I won't. You're quite devious, you know."

"Yes, but at least I'm using my powers for good. This time." Taryn winked at her, then gestured at the orange cat that had somehow shifted another two ledges over until he was nearly sitting at the table with them. She hadn't noticed him move at all. "Are you going to sic Ninja Cat on me because of this?"

"I should," Bonnie said, but she laughed, looking more relaxed now. "His name is Salmon, and he's very gentle but aloof. He's hovering because he loves Sasha, not because he wants to eviscerate you."

"Salmon?" Taryn repeated. She really needed to get back out of that habit.

"Yes, well, salmon have a lot of significance in the Northwest. They're an important part of our local ecosystems, just like *he* is in our café."

"You have a tell," Taryn said when Bonnie faltered to a stop after her weak explanation. Taryn waggled her finger between her own eyes. "You squint when you're lying. You did the same thing when you said you were certain there were no cats in the kitchen."

"I said cats weren't allowed in the kitchen," Bonnie clarified with an indignant look that only lasted a few seconds before she laughed. "Oh, all right. I had salmon for dinner the night before my friend brought him to the café, and his coloring kind of looks salmon-like. Go ahead and laugh, but you try naming up to ten cats a month. You run out of clever ideas and just start going with the first thing that comes to mind."

Taryn leaned forward conspiratorially, careful not to dislodge Sasha. "So, are there actually cats in the kitchen?"

"No. Definitely not. Well, probably not, but it's not an impossibility." She scanned the room. "I'm eighty percent sure there aren't, but if I could find Kip…Oh, there he is." She pointed at a small black cat sunning himself on a windowsill. "Okay, I'll go up to ninety percent sure."

Chapter Eight

Bonnie finished the afternoon baking the next day, then wandered through the café picking up toys and rearranging empty tables until Isa finally told her to stop fussing and just go. She lingered a little longer, checking on the kittens and adding some items to her running grocery list, then finally took Isa's advice and started the walk back to her house where her car was parked.

She still had time before she had to be at Taryn's office to sign the rental agreement and discuss wedding plans. Taryn had scheduled the meeting and left the café soon after Bonnie accepted her offer to plan an adoption event as a bonus for Bonnie agreeing to host Marty and Lex's wedding, as if she expected Bonnie to change her mind and wanted to leave before it could happen.

Taryn needn't have worried, though. Bonnie wasn't about to turn down the opportunity to not only share information about the adoption process and find homes for some of her cats, but also to help her friends who had rescue groups and were always struggling to find fosters and adopters. She decided to wait until the date and details were finalized before telling Nancy. Otherwise she might show up at the café days ahead of time with a U-Haul stuffed to the roof with cats.

The main reason Bonnie wasn't going to back out of the deal, though, was because she had already decided to say yes the next time Taryn asked. As hard as she had tried to find a reasonable excuse for standing her ground and refusing to host the wedding, her only arguments were weak ones that skirted her real issue with the event.

Such as her avoidance of things associated with marriages because they represented her family's expectations for all its offspring.

Or her reluctance to face the intensified familial badgering she'd receive if her café turned into a singles destination.

While those reasons were perfectly valid for her and were far from exaggerations about her family's likely response to the situation, they were insignificant to the cats or to her business, especially when compared to how both the cats and the business would benefit if she agreed to the wedding.

And, truth be told, her younger self had been far more upset by her family's badgering than she was now. Now she just felt mildly annoyed at the prospect.

All she had to do was stay as far out of the picture as possible. Literally. She could stay in the kitchen while the press took photos and could hide out in the upstairs room if guests were being interviewed. The focus would be on Lex and Marty, and she'd make sure none of the attention strayed too close to her.

She had come to terms with her eventual submission to Taryn's request—though not delving too deeply into her inclination to submit to Taryn's flirting, too, if it happened again. Still, she had been surprised to see Taryn back at the café so soon and had still been reluctant, if resigned, to let this highly publicized event happen in her café, so Taryn made her enticing offer before she had a chance to tell Taryn she'd changed her mind.

Bonnie paused for a moment on a street corner, admiring the garden that was her favorite part of her daily walks to and from the café. The mingling scents from dozens of types of flowering plants made a gentle perfume in the air that always soothed her when she was feeling anxious.

She thought back to the question she had asked Taryn yesterday, about whether she was there to argue for the wedding or to flirt with Bonnie again. It had turned out to be the former, despite Taryn's protests to the contrary, but Bonnie would have found the latter even more enticing and hard to decline. Apparently the flirting had just been part of the attempt to get Bonnie's signature on the rental contract. Which was a shame, since Taryn intrigued her with her unpredictable humor and clever mind. And her skin. When she had touched Bonnie's arm, she had felt as if all her attention, all her blood and nerve endings, were straining toward that one small patch on her arm where Taryn's hand rested.

Bonnie started walking again, moving away from the romantic spring aroma that seemed to be messing with her mind and her common sense. It was fortunate that Taryn hadn't been at the café for personal reasons, not a shame. It was a relief. Not exactly a flattering one, though...

Bonnie pulled out her phone to call her brother. She had found that the best way to make any problem in her life seem less dire was to get in touch with a family member. Plus, she had been meaning to call him since the morning her mother had given her the news about the second wedding. She had intended to contact him that day, but then Taryn had walked into her life, bringing unwelcome weddings and romance onto Bonnie's turf. To put it mildly, she hadn't been in a suitable frame of mind for gushing over his impending nuptials. Or renuptials?

"Hey, sis," he said when he answered. Bonnie could hear

the voices, bangs, and laughter in the background that always made up the drone from his chaotic home life.

"Hey, Jonah," she said. "Mom told me the good news. Congratulations. I was amazed you got Mayu to say yes once, let alone twice."

"Me, too!" he agreed with a laugh. "To tell you the truth, I was a little worried to ask again. Like maybe I just caught her on a good day the first time, and she's been waiting for a chance to reconsider."

She laughed along with him. She could joke with him about managing to snare the sought-after former pageant queen and current local television star because she knew how much they loved each other. Mayu had lucked out in the deal, too. Jonah might be the quieter counterpoint to her public persona, but he had been more than content to support her and let her shine. When their parents weren't around and Jonah wasn't trying desperately to grasp at any approval crumbs they offered, he was not just a brother, but one of her closest friends. When their parents were around, she felt a little sorry for him and how hard he tried to keep their attention.

"So, another elaborate wedding, hmm?" Bonnie asked as she got to her house and unlocked her car. She could have just driven to work instead of doing her usual walk, but she seemed to be desperately searching for ways to delay her trip to Taryn's office. If she didn't hurry now, though, she would be late.

"Yes, although I forgot how exhausting the first one was to organize. Today is all about flowers and table settings. We're heading to the wedding planner's office in a little while."

Bonnie dropped her keys between her seat and the center console, and she fumbled for them as she half listened to Jonah talk. She didn't feel sorry for him since he had voluntarily chosen to repeat his wedding. She fished her keys out of the narrow gap and spoke without thinking through her next words.

"Funny. I'm doing the same thing today."

"You're going to a... You're getting married? Mayu, come here. Bonnie's getting married!"

"No, no, no, no," Bonnie repeated even though no one was on the other end of the line to hear her. Damn it.

"Why didn't you tell us?" Jonah demanded when he came back. Bonnie could hear the excited murmur of Mayu asking questions of her own in the background. "Who is she? When can we meet her?"

"I'm not getting married, Jonah, so please tell me you're not texting Mom right now. I'm going to see a wedding planner because Sumner's mayor is getting married in my café."

"You're not getting married. She's not getting married," he repeated, in a more muffled voice, probably because he was aiming the comment at Mayu. "The mayor, sis? That's a big deal."

"The mayor of *Sumner*," she said, emphasizing her town's name. He sounded genuinely impressed by her news, so she assumed he hadn't registered the city in his excitement over her false wedding. "Martin Hannah. He met his partner Lex at the café, and they adopted two cats."

"Wow. That's really...wow. Mayu interviewed him just a couple of months ago. She was really impressed by him."

Now she was going to be really late. She switched to speaker and clipped her phone into a holder on her dash. At least she didn't have time to stew about this appointment on her way to Taryn's since she spent the entire drive fielding questions from Mayu and Jonah. All she really knew about Marty and Lex was the names of their cats, so she didn't have many satisfactory answers for them. When she pulled into the parking lot next to Taryn's small office complex, she ended the call, promising Jonah she would keep him updated on the wedding plans. He and Mayu had seemed more excited about the wedding of a small-town mayor than their own.

She put the call out of her mind—not easy to do since she knew Jonah was probably on the phone and spreading her news to the rest of the family. She would eagerly await the *You're having a wedding in your café? Too bad you're not the one getting married* calls she was sure to receive tonight.

❖

Taryn's office was just off Meridian, on the hill between the Puyallup fairgrounds and the South Hill Mall. The location was prime, and easy to find. Bonnie had worried about parking, but the lot attached to the strip of offices was nearly empty, and she was able to find a spot directly in front of Taryn's door. She walked into an empty reception area, with a small desk in the center and several comfortable love seats and chairs lining the walls. A door on the far side of the room was marked by a burnished gold plate with Taryn's name on it in black lettering, and Taryn herself came out to greet Bonnie as soon as she stepped inside.

"Hello," she said, remaining in her doorway. "Come on back."

Bonnie crossed the room and followed Taryn into her office. She was wearing a similar style of clothing as she had on her visits to the café and otherwise looked the same on the surface, but there was something different about her in this setting. Her smile was friendly enough, but she seemed every inch the professional in a borderline distant way. Bonnie wasn't sure if this was her true self and the playful, outgoing Taryn she had met in the café was just an act, or vice versa.

She walked through the doorway and paused, captivated

by the hundreds of photos lining every wall. She slowly circled the room, looking at each picture in turn. Taryn stood patiently next to her desk as Bonnie walked around her, apparently accustomed to having everyone who entered the office do the same thing.

Bonnie had been to dozens of weddings for family and friends, and had stood stiff and smiling in plenty of wedding photos. The couples and bridal parties, color schemes and floral arrangements had been different in each one, but there had been a thread of sameness running through them all.

If Bonnie had been shown all the photos from weddings she had attended with the newlywed couples erased, she would only have been able to identify whose wedding it was based on the process of elimination, ruling out the ushers and bridesmaids.

But each of Taryn's pictures was one of a kind, reflecting the unique ceremonies they captured. Some details were traditional, like the brides who were wearing big white dresses, but instead of standing on church steps next to an arch of white roses, they were dangling from rock climbing walls or water skiing. One was riding a mechanical bull.

She saw quite a few animals in the photos, too. Horses and dogs and goats that seemed to play significant roles in the ceremonies. One man was holding a cat wearing a bejeweled harness.

But there was nothing like Bonnie's café. Marty and Lex's photo was going to be something special.

She finished her circuit of the room and faced Taryn again. Bonnie had her reasons—valid reasons—for wanting to keep the wedding out of her café, but she had to admire Taryn for fighting her. She wasn't doing it to punish Bonnie, but to give Marty and Lex a truly special day. The day *they* wanted.

She would have been much happier if their desires hadn't

become such a pain in her ass, but the thought of how happy she and Taryn were going to make them helped a little. "You did this," she said. "You made all these dreams come true."

Taryn was silent for a moment, then she nodded. "I did." The two simple words held a note of pride that softened her businesslike demeanor by a fraction. Bonnie's cats meant everything to her, and they made her work feel like a true calling and not just a job. She sensed that Taryn felt the same enthusiasm for her career. It showed in the photos, and even more in the expression on her face when she looked at them.

Bonnie tried to ignore the sense of connection the acknowledgment of their similarities made her feel toward Taryn, focusing instead on her annoyance over the whole wedding business. Somehow, though, while standing in this room where weddings seemed to reflect personalities and passion more than society's expectations, her annoyance was too slippery to grasp.

She dragged her attention off Taryn and pointed at one of the pictures. It featured a couple standing on a rocky ledge with a panoramic view of trees and mountain peaks stretched behind them. Bonnie thought she recognized Mount St. Helens in the background. Judging by the ropes attached to the cliff face below them and the harnesses they wore over their tuxedos, they had climbed their way to the ceremony site. "That looks steep," she said. "Did you have to climb up with them to get the picture?"

"Not all the way to the altar. Their friend who officiated is an experienced climber, too, so just the three of them went up the cliff. The rest of us remained at its base, but we had a good view of the ceremony."

Taryn came up behind Bonnie as she spoke until she was standing right beside her. Close enough that they would touch if Bonnie took too deep a breath. Luckily, Taryn's closeness made her inhalations shallower than normal.

"Still, the climb the rest of the guests and I had to make to get there was challenging, especially since most of us were novices," Taryn continued. She reached out and ran one finger along the frame, straightening the photo just a fraction of an inch. "It was worth the effort. The air was so clear we could hear every word they said."

"It looks like it was a beautiful ceremony," Bonnie said, nudging Taryn with her shoulder, bridging the distance between them in spite of herself. "Have you suggested it as an option to Marty and Lex? They might be able to rig up little harnesses for Tango and Rumba since they're so intent on having cats at their wedding."

"Nice try," Taryn said with a laugh, leaning into Bonnie's shoulder slightly before easing away. "But the only climbing they're interested in doing is up the stairs leading to your café. Come on, let's get this paperwork done."

Bonnie sat down next to the desk, and Taryn slid a slender black portfolio in front of her.

"Let's take care of the contract for the adoption event first," Taryn said, probably thinking Bonnie would refuse to sign anything else until she had Taryn locked into planning her event. In truth, after seeing the photos, she felt a growing excitement to see what magic Taryn would create for her cats.

Taryn slowly went through the contract, explaining every detail before she asked Bonnie to sign.

"Finding Furever," Bonnie said, reading the name off the top of the contract.

Taryn hesitated before speaking. "I thought it might be a good name for the event, but it can just be a placeholder if you want something different."

"No," Bonnie assured her. It was a cute name and captured exactly what Bonnie wanted for her cats and their potential adopters. She was tempted to sign immediately but couldn't bring herself to do it without being completely honest with Taryn. "It's perfect. I love it. It's just...I should tell you that I had already decided to let Marty and Lex have their wedding in the café even before you suggested this event. It really sounds wonderful, but you don't need to—"

"Sign there, and initial the highlighted spaces." Taryn interrupted her, pointing at a line on the last page.

Bonnie hesitated, but Taryn just watched her with a steadily inscrutable expression, so she reached for the pen Taryn offered with a sigh of relief. She had been getting excited about the possibilities the event provided her and her animals, almost enough to make the rest of the bargain worthwhile. At least at the adoption event, no press would be likely to show, and the guests would be paying attention mostly to the cats. No one would care about her or her past.

She and Taryn both signed the contract, and then Taryn made a copy for her before bringing out the rental agreement for the café.

"The rental fee doesn't include catering costs," Taryn said, tapping her pen on the line with the amount Bonnie would make. "They'll most likely want heavy hors d'oeuvres and a dessert table, but we can discuss your fees once the menu is set. Does the rental cost seem fair to you?"

"It'll do," Bonnie said, fighting to keep her voice neutral even though she felt like getting up and dancing around the room. She was going to change her place's name to Bonnie's Love Café and have a wedding there every weekend.

Okay, maybe not.

But the price they were paying made the idea very

tempting. With what she had already saved, this put her very close to getting her tearoom addition built.

Taryn grinned at her, looking more like she had at the café as she seemed to easily gauge Bonnie's true reaction to the money she would make. "Marty and Lex specifically told me not to lowball you with their offer, but even so, this is close to the going rate. You need to be compensated for the income you're missing by closing to the public for a day, on top of the fee to rent your café. If you decide to have other events there in the future—nonromantic, nonwedding events, of course— then don't accept much less than this, okay?"

Bonnie nodded, struggling to process everything that was happening. Having this publicized wedding, with reporters and guests posting every moment on social media, in her café still felt uncomfortable to her. Not enough for her to deny Marty and Lex their dream wedding day or to turn down money that would provide much needed help for food and vet bills, but disconcerting enough that she would need time to think this over and decide how to handle similar situations in the future. For now, though, she signed the contract.

"Excellent," Taryn said, nearly snatching the papers out from under Bonnie's pen as she finished her signature. "We'll work out most of the details in the coming weeks, but today I'd like to go over a few specific requests Marty and Lex have, as well as some of my own ideas."

"All right," Bonnie said warily. She had assumed that the day wouldn't be much different from any other at the café, aside from the fact that a couple of the patrons would say vows at some point during the evening and people might be dressed a little more formally than her usual clientele. Otherwise, business as usual.

Taryn opened a leather binder and flipped a couple of

pages. "The ceremony is taking place on October thirtieth, so the wedding will have a Halloween theme, with the main colors of purple and silver. Think elegant Halloween, not kitschy Halloween."

"Okay." Bonnie frowned. "What exactly makes it elegant?"

Taryn turned the binder around to face Bonnie and flipped through some pictures of cats wearing bow ties. A few even had on Halloween costumes and funny hats. She pointed at one of the photos. "Something like this. I thought the cats could wear little purple bow ties and cummerbunds. Maybe some of them could have rhinestone capes instead, to provide a visual contrast."

Bonnie imagined wrangling all her cats into ties, like the cranky looking ones in the photos. She'd be ripped to shreds. "You want them to wear clothes?"

"It's a formal wedding," Taryn said, as if that answered Bonnie's question. It didn't. "And since black cats are associated with Halloween, I thought we could have as many of those near the altar as possible during the ceremony."

"Kip and Chummy are the only black cats we have right now, but I don't know how you expect me to make them stand at the altar for more than two seconds." She'd be darting in and out of the ceremony, scooping up cats and carrying them back to their assigned places. Again…ripped to shreds.

"Only two black cats," Taryn said thoughtfully, making a note on the page. "Are you opposed to dyeing some of the others? It doesn't need to be permanent, of course. Just a semipermanent color rinse."

Bonnie opened her mouth to respond to Taryn's request, but no sound came out. She wanted to grab the contract and rip it up, but Taryn had tucked it out of sight in her desk the moment Bonnie had signed it. She was sure she hadn't seen anything written in there about coloring her cats' fur.

"Do they sing?" Taryn continued, flipping to a new page. "You know, meow when you play music?"

This was ridiculous. Bonnie didn't care how much Marty and Lex were paying. She wasn't hosting a circus in her café. "Are you serious? What do you want them to do, meow the 'Wedding March'?"

"No, of course not," Taryn said with a scoffing laugh. "Nothing so traditional. I was thinking something more modern and edgy. Oh, do they rap?"

"Do they *rap*?" Bonnie repeated.

These requests were ludicrous. Taryn couldn't possibly expect her to agree to any of these suggestions, but she was watching Bonnie with a serenely serious expression, one neat eyebrow slightly raised. Well, she wasn't going to stand for...

Bonnie paused.

Was Taryn looking a little too calm, given Bonnie's obvious—and most likely highly visible—reluctance to go along with her plans?

"You actually *don't* expect me to agree to any of this, do you," Bonnie stated, continuing her inner monologue out loud. She watched Taryn with a mixture of awe and annoyance. "You're even more devious than I thought. You want me to hate these ridiculous ideas because then I'll agree to anything even remotely reasonable out of sheer relief that I'm not dressing my cats in prom wear or dipping them in a vat of black dye."

"I have no idea what you're talking about," Taryn said, her composed mask slipping a little and revealing a hint of a smile. "But if you don't like any of my suggestions, then I'm sure we can come to some sort of"—she waved one of her elegant hands carelessly in the air—"compromise."

"Compromise, my ass," Bonnie said, fighting to keep from laughing. "You know exactly what you want, and you just tried to condition me to not only accept your plan, but to be grateful for whatever it is."

"Did it work?" Taryn asked.

"Probably," Bonnie admitted. "But you still deserve to be punished for acting in such an unprofessional manner. I'm going to buy a fish costume, so next time you come to the café, you can try putting it on Salmon. Bring a first aid kit."

CHAPTER NINE

Taryn set her decoy binder to one side and took out the real one, with her sketched-out ideas for the wedding. She had figured Bonnie would see through her ploy eventually. She had caught on quicker than Taryn expected, but still, the mental pictures her outrageous suggestions had planted in Bonnie's mind would have to make every subsequent idea seem downright pleasant.

She had suspected that Bonnie would eventually agree to the wedding, but her admission—before she signed the cat event contract and not after, no less—disarmed Taryn. How easy it would have been for her to back out, and to minimize her contact with Bonnie, the café, and all its feline residents, but she hadn't even hesitated before insisting they go through with the deal.

Her business was doing well, and she was in a good place to give back to her local community by helping some worthy charities in a completely selfless way that would leave her covered in cat fur and possibly covered with welts like Angie's. The selfish desire to spend a little more time in Bonnie's company was a mere afterthought to the real reason she had kept to their original bargain, of course.

She was doing this for the cats. Really.

She couldn't completely sell that line of reasoning to herself, and she knew Angie would fall over laughing when she heard about it. Taryn decided to ignore introspection about her motivation and just keep moving forward. The contract was signed. She was committed. Or should be committed…

One of the two.

Taryn flipped open the binder to a page with woefully few pictures of cat toys and moved it so Bonnie could see. "The color scheme really is purple and silver. I had been thinking we could exchange your cat toys for ones in those colors, but I wasn't able to find many when I searched online. I'll have to keep looking." She paused and glanced at Bonnie, who was leaning toward her and frowning at the page. Maybe Taryn's plan hadn't worked as well as she'd hoped, and Bonnie was still determined to fight her every step of the way.

"You hate the idea. You're making a face."

"I'm not making a face," Bonnie said indignantly. "I was just thinking. It's a clever way to decorate since we can't have a lot of flowers the cats will eat or decorations they'll destroy, but you're right that you won't find many options in the right colors. We can get ribbons and feathers and make our own."

"Really?" Taryn asked, caught off guard by the suggestion.

Bonnie laughed. "We can even use part of your pretend wedding plans. A lot of our cats like chasing little felt mice, so I have a ton of them. We can put tiny purple bow ties on them and scatter them around the café."

Taryn grinned. "Perfect. They can be wedding favors for guests that have cats. The rest you can keep, or we can donate them after the ceremony."

Bonnie smiled at that, then bit her lip and settled back in her chair again, still seeming ready to be on the defensive, as if Taryn's next request would be to spray-paint red hearts on the sides of her cats.

"So, what else?" she asked.

"The menu," Taryn said. "It has to be all pumpkin."

"All pumpkin?" She gave a laugh that sounded forced to Taryn. "Is this another joke, like the musical meows?"

"No, sorry. This one is real."

Bonnie bit her lip, which would have been more enticing to watch if Taryn wasn't still on high alert, expecting Bonnie to bolt at any moment, contract be damned.

"What does that mean, exactly?"

Taryn gave in to the urge she had been feeling ever since Marty and Lex had told her about this part and rolled her eyes. In all her time as a wedding planner, she'd never had a request for a one-ingredient menu. "I have no idea. This is your area of expertise, as the official wedding caterer. Apparently, they started talking at the café because they each had the same color cat on their laps and were both drinking pumpkin spice lattes. It's a very adorable story of two people who were destined to meet." At least according to Marty and Lex. They had used the word *adorable* no less than six times in their first meeting with her, so she was going to take their word for it.

"Yeah. Destiny," Bonnie said, with a sniff. "The odds of two customers having that particular drink in a coffee shop in the fall are astronomical."

"Cynic," Taryn said with a smirk. "At least this gives you a way to keep budding romances to a minimum in the café. Just make sure only one person at a time orders each drink, so none of them can try to bond over a shared love of meow-chas. Say, what silly name do you give PSLs anyway?"

"I don't give them a silly name," Bonnie said, squinting slightly. She caught herself with a laugh and rubbed the bridge of her nose. "Oh, all right. Pawmpkin Spice. Stop laughing. I could probably support the café on those drinks alone from September to December. So, purple cat toys and an all-pumpkin menu. Sounds like every other wedding I've ever been to so far. Is there anything else?"

"Very funny. I can guarantee this will be a one-of-a-kind event. I'd like to bring them by the café sometime soon for a tasting, and we can go over more details when they're actually in the space. Oh, and they'll need a room where they can get ready before the ceremony."

"They can use the kitten room," Bonnie said, idly turning pages in Taryn's binder.

The entries were scarce at this stage of the planning, and it was little more than a vision board right now. Taryn rarely let anyone see her work this early in the process, even the people involved in the wedding. She was torn between wanting to grab the book from Bonnie and wanting to ask her what she thought of the images Taryn had collected.

"Really? A room full of kittens?" she asked, Bonnie's words finally penetrating her mind. She had been too focused on the intimacy of sharing this nascent part of her creativity with another person and had almost missed the meaning of her words.

"Well, there are six that live there right now, but it varies. It's basically a main suite with a large bedroom and bathroom. I can put the kittens in another room while they—"

"No," Taryn said, holding up a hand to stop her. She could imagine their faces when she gave them this bit of news. "They'll nominate me for wedding planner of the year if they get kittens in their dressing room. It'll probably be the highlight of their night."

"Fine," said Bonnie. "Just not too much traffic in there."

"I promise," Taryn said. "We'll keep access limited. There's a good chance, though, that we might not be able to get them to leave the room and come downstairs. And we'll need to check their pockets before they go home, or you might find yourself with one or two fewer kittens at the end of the night."

Taryn fidgeted with her pen. They had covered the only requirements she had at the moment.

She had sent Angie to the mall to pick up some supplies, wanting to keep her out of the office while Bonnie was there. She had absolutely no doubt that Angie would have brought up Taryn's deficient flirting skills or something equally embarrassing once she found out who Bonnie was. Taryn was feeling frayed around the edges as it was, having Bonnie here in her personal space. Yes, it was her work office, but it often felt more personal and expressive of who she was than her own home did. Taryn was making more of an effort than usual to remain professional and composed, and she didn't think she could maintain the facade if Angie was here joking about her divorce and Taryn's nonexistent love life.

So what she needed to do was shoo Bonnie along now that the contracts were signed and the initial details ironed out.

"What made you change your mind?" she found herself asking instead. "About the wedding. You said you'd already decided to say yes the next time I asked."

"Oh, well, I don't know…" Bonnie said. She closed the binder and carefully lined it up with the edge of the desk. Taryn could practically see her mentally inventing excuses then rejecting them before she seemed to decide to tell the truth. No squinting.

"My reasons for saying no had more to do with me than with what's good for the café or what's right to do for Marty and Lex." She shrugged as if none of this really mattered to her, but Taryn knew better. Some part of this wedding was obviously an emotional trigger for her.

"I'm the youngest of six kids, and my parents raised us to see only two options in life," Bonnie continued. "Marriage with a huge family, or a job with a huge income. I chose a different path when I went to work with rescue groups, and that eventually led me here. A job with a tiny income and no family besides my friends and my cats. I'm happy with my life, but they still believe something is missing from it, and I know that any connections between my café and romance will make them more zealous about pushing me toward marriage and a *Brady Bunch* number of kids. But it's nothing I can't handle with more than an occasional headache, so saying no to the wedding seemed petty and selfish."

Taryn had a feeling there was more to this than Bonnie's parents saying they wanted grandchildren or for their daughter to have an impressive financial portfolio to have made her fight so hard against the idea of a wedding at her café.

She could almost see the point at which Bonnie's explanation moved from truth to something tangential to it— somewhere in the transition from her previous jobs to that of café owner. She didn't seem to be lying, but holding something back.

They still didn't know each other well. Taryn hoped that sometime between now and the wedding she might earn Bonnie's trust enough to know her full story, but for now she accepted the reason she was given and latched on to the part of it that resonated with her.

"Funny," she said, with a laugh that didn't have any humor behind it. "My parents told me basically the opposite when they argued, which was pretty much all the time. *Don't ever get married, Taryn, because he'll never help around the house.* And from the other side, *This is why you shouldn't get married because she'll criticize every damned thing you do.*"

Taryn paused, surprised at herself for saying any of that out loud. She had even done fair imitations of her mother and father, which usually only happened in her head and never in front of another person. She had been hoping things might evolve to be more personal between them, and when her guard was down, Taryn had in turn shared more of her past than usual.

Even though she had only spoken two disparaging remarks of all the ones she had heard regularly when she was younger, she still felt as exposed as if she had just handed Bonnie a three-hundred-page memoir. She didn't talk about her childhood with anyone.

"And so you became a wedding planner. Neither of us listened to our parents very well, did we?"

Bonnie's smile was rueful, with no sign of mocking or teasing in her voice, but Taryn tried to turn her comment into a joke. Anything to get them back to the casual realm rather than the more emotional one Taryn had unwittingly led them to with her probing of Bonnie's reasons for fighting against the wedding.

"I guess I'm just the rebellious type," she said, keeping her tone light and a smile on her face.

"Hmm. All right," Bonnie said.

"All right what?" Taryn asked, more sharply than she had intended. So much for the unflustered attitude she had been trying to impart.

"All right, I believe you." Bonnie held up her hands in mock surrender. "You chose this job just to spite them." She paused and gave a small shrug with one shoulder, as if expressing an afterthought. "I only thought there might be another reason."

Taryn crossed her arms over her chest, then deliberately

relaxed her forearms back onto her desk when she realized how defensive she looked—just as self-protective as Bonnie had been when Taryn had originally approached her about the wedding, unintentionally bringing an uncomfortable situation into her café. "Let's hear it, then," she said with as much indifference as she could muster.

Bonnie leaned toward her, speaking quietly as if understanding that what they were discussing was something private, something Taryn wouldn't want to be spread beyond this office. "Well, maybe you couldn't fix your parents' marriage, so you try to make as many other couples as possible happy. If they have this wonderful day that binds them together as who they are, and not what anyone else expects them to be, then you're giving their marriages a better chance to succeed."

Taryn paused, surprised by how well Bonnie had summed up her situation in a few dozen words. Taryn herself rarely examined her own reasons for choosing her career this closely. She preferred to pretend she wasn't still reacting to the fights and hurtful words from her childhood, when she had taken every critical comment made by either parent and had tried to solve the problem.

"I suppose you're a tiny bit correct," she said, realizing that Bonnie had just done to her what she tried to do for all her clients. To make them feel seen and heard and *known* by someone. Validation was a heady feeling, and it threatened to make her lower her guard even more. "I tried to fix whatever they were fighting about, as if it would make them love each other again. When they argued about which one wasn't cooking often enough, I stepped in and started making dinner every night. When they yelled about who wasn't doing enough housework, I made myself a cleaning schedule and took over most of the chores. None of it worked, of course, since I was trying to solve the surface issues, and was far too young to understand any of the subtext behind their arguments. I became a highly organized child, though. I think that might be as much of what led me to a career in event planning as anything else. I'm destined to organize, which doesn't sound nearly as sexy as being a rebel."

Bonnie laughed and sat up, breaking the sense of closeness Taryn had been feeling as they had been leaning toward each other.

"That Bad Boy or Bad Girl image is overrated, if you ask me. I spend my days juggling running a business and feeding dozens of cats and customers. Someone who knows her way around an hourly planner is sexier than a rebel any day."

"Really? Well, then, wait until you see my Excel spreadsheets," Taryn said, swiveling her laptop to face Bonnie.

"Whoa. I barely know you," Bonnie said, standing up and shielding her eyes as she backed toward the door. "Let's keep things professional, please."

Taryn laughed. "Fine. I'll be bringing Lex and Marty to the café on Friday. We can discuss timetables and detailed task lists for the wedding and the adoption event."

"Enough organizational talk. You're making me blush."

Bonnie waved good-bye, then left the office. Taryn turned her laptop around again, but instead of getting back to work, she rehashed her conversation with Bonnie in her mind. They had taken care of the necessary business of contracts and initial planning, which was good. Not so good was Taryn's unexpected spate of oversharing.

Bonnie had made it all right, though. She had listened and understood. Then she had managed to turn the conversation in a playful direction just when Taryn had had enough personal talk. She was going to have to watch herself carefully until the two events involving Bonnie's cat café were finished and they had parted ways. Because while she agreed with Angie that her own flirting skills were weak from disuse, Bonnie's were dangerously effective and might take every ounce of Taryn's resolve to resist.

CHAPTER TEN

Bonnie got back to the café in time to help Jerome arrange the tea trays for the afternoon guests. After her meeting with Taryn, she had been looking forward to having such a routine and predictable task to focus her mind and keep her from dwelling on the afternoon's conversation. Unfortunately, that same predictability meant she could lay out the items with perfect precision even while proverbially juggling kittens, so she found herself placing crustless sandwiches on the tiered trays while thinking of nothing but Taryn.

She was more changeable than anyone Bonnie knew— switching from cool professional to trickster to wounded child without any gradual steps between. But instead of feeling left behind by Taryn's sudden swings, Bonnie had felt comfortable with them, somehow knowing when Taryn had hidden things to share and when she needed Bonnie to back off and let her be. Taryn was interesting and complex, and every side she showed Bonnie seemed just as genuine as the last. Bonnie found herself more intrigued by her than she should be.

It didn't help that Taryn seemed as fascinating physically as she was intellectually. She was strong, no doubt. In their short acquaintance, Bonnie had managed to touch her thigh and, yesterday, her arm when their shoulders had brushed against each other. Even if it had been a while since she'd had sex, she was quite capable of recognizing muscles when she felt them. Taryn's strength was balanced by a graceful elegance in her gestures and movements. Bonnie spent far too much of their time together inventing excuses to touch Taryn more.

Bonnie pulled herself back to the present and scooped homemade strawberry-rhubarb jam into little glass dishes and set them next to the scones on the second tiers. The batch had turned out well, but she'd get even better results in June, during the short period when the two ingredients were available fresh at the same time. The store-bought cultivated berries she had to use in early spring were never as flavorful as the ones direct from local farms.

She finished the last tray just as Jerome came into the kitchen to help her carry them upstairs. These teas ran like clockwork, with the only variable being provided by unpredictable kittens. That sort of chaos was always welcome.

"Everyone's settled in, except the kittens. They're bouncing off the walls." Jerome laughed. "Literally. They're chasing the shadows of leaves from the window and bouncing off the walls."

Bonnie smiled. She was always happy when the kittens were in a mood to be entertaining for the customers. Not that anyone had ever complained when they preferred to curl up in the tearoom guests' laps and take naps. They were a hit with everyone no matter what they did.

"I had an idea for the website," she said as she and Jerome picked up the trays by their handles and carefully edged out of the kitchen. "What about setting up a webcam in the kitten room? People can watch them on the website, and it would be good advertisement for the teas."

"That would be amazing," he said, leading the way up

the stairs. "You know, we should put another one in the main room. That sunny spot near the window seat always has a bunch of cats, and if we keep some of their toys there, we might get more activity. We can keep the angles low so it'll be more cat-focused, and I'll make signs to post so customers can avoid those areas if they choose."

"Great. I'll get the equipment we need this weekend," Bonnie said, not sure why she suddenly felt reluctant to do something that was not only her idea, but was sure to be popular with visitors to the website and to regular customers who might enjoy checking in on their furry friends when they couldn't come see them. It should be easy for her to avoid being on screen at all, but she would have to be more self-aware than she usually was when she wandered through her café.

Taryn was to blame for this new brainstorm of Bonnie's. Her reaction to using the kitten room as a prep area for the wedding had made Bonnie wish more people could have access to the room without overwhelming its occupants.

Taryn again.

Bonnie really needed to find a new obsession.

❖

That resolution lasted about fifteen minutes, and then Bonnie found herself on the phone, waiting for Taryn to pick up. She was torn between wanting to berate herself for being weak and feeling indulgent toward herself. Her time with Taryn would be limited to the adoption event and the wedding, so why not add some extra moments when she had the chance? She doubted Taryn would have much cause to rent out a cat café again in the future, and Bonnie still was undecided about whether she'd ever say yes to another ceremony after this one if the opportunity was offered no matter how great the money was.

The phone rang several times, and Bonnie had decided to hang up as soon as she was sent to voice mail, but Taryn answered.

"Hello?"

"Hi. It's Bonnie."

"I know," Taryn said, and Bonnie could hear the humor in her voice. "Your name showed up on my screen. What's up?"

Bonnie rested her forehead against the wall next to the kitchen door as she tried to pull herself together. She had made her way through plenty of phone conversations without sounding like a fool. This one shouldn't be any different.

"I'm going to a farm my friends own in the Valley tomorrow afternoon," she said. "I need to pick up some produce, and I wanted to talk to them about what will be in season in October. Get some ideas for the wedding menu. I… well, I was wondering if you'd want to come along. Offer some suggestions about what Lex and Marty might like, that sort of thing. I'd understand if you're too busy. Plus, it's supposed to rain tonight, so we'd be slogging around in the mud."

Taryn laughed. It was a soft sound, as if she was trying not to be overheard. "I appreciate you giving me some valid excuses so I can decline, but I don't need them. I'd love to go. So I can oversee the menu planning, of course, because it's part of my job as wedding planner."

Bonnie exhaled. She hadn't realized she'd been holding her breath until Taryn said yes, and suddenly she could breathe again. "Is it also part of your job to come up with a full menu of pumpkin dishes?"

"No, that's all on you. To be honest, I figured you'd just put out some platters of pumpkin pie and maybe pumpkin muffins."

"Ha. We'll be able to do better than that. And remember, when you announce each dish to the guests, you need to call it *pawmpkin*."

"That will definitely not happen." Taryn paused. "It's still early afternoon. Where are you?"

"In the café."

"In the kitchen?" Taryn lowered her voice to a conspiratorial whisper. "Is a cat in there with you?"

Bonnie looked over and saw Kip sitting on the counter, licking his paw and using it to clean his whiskers. "No," she said. "Absolutely not."

"Sure. I don't even need to video chat and see your face to know you're lying. Is it the little black one? Remember, you need to be training him to stand at the altar while they say their vows. Maybe he can hand them the wedding rings."

Bonnie laughed. "I can't even train him to stay in the main room, so we're far from doling out jewelry. Chummy is pretty smart, though. I might be able to teach him to strew flower petals along the aisle in front of Marty and Lex."

Bonnie was rewarded with a burst of laughter from Taryn—this one not quiet enough to keep from being overheard by anyone near her.

They set a time to meet the following day, and then Bonnie picked up Kip and sneaked him back into the main room without any customers noticing. She hoped he'd find a forever home soon, where he could hang out in his new owner's kitchen whenever he wanted.

❖

The next day, Taryn slid into Bonnie's passenger seat and smiled at her as she buckled her seat belt. "Good afternoon," she said. "There are quite a few more cars out here than I've seen parked here before. Are you sure you can be away from the café if it's busy?"

Bonnie nosed her car out of the tight parking place and drove toward Main Street. "I do mornings alone at least once a week, and Isa and Jerome are both here in the afternoon. It gives me a chance to do some shopping, and to get to the farm in spring and summer." She glanced over at Taryn, who was wearing faded jeans and a sweatshirt with the sleeves rolled up. She even had on ankle boots that looked like they could withstand at least a few inches of mud. Bonnie hadn't yet seen Taryn this casual, and even her posture and demeanor seemed more relaxed out of her work clothes.

"What kind of farm is this going to be?" Taryn asked. "I've had weddings at orchards and big horse farms, but nothing local."

"Ben and Daisy have a little of everything," Bonnie said. She had met them at a farmers market when she had first opened her café, and they had connected with each other because of a shared passion for using local, fresh ingredients. She had gone to the farm to visit and had bonded with them over bowls of just-picked berries cooled with specks of fresh mint. "They have fruit trees, berry bushes, and tons of space for growing vegetables. They also produce honey and all sorts of goat milk products. They open their pumpkin patch to the public every fall, so I'll get the wedding dinner pumpkins from them. We could get some for decorations, too."

She paused and pointed at a sign they were passing for The Old Cannery. The warehouse-style store sold furnishings with an emphasis on Northwest-inspired styles. They also had an unexpected case full of fudge for sale.

"Look," she said. "It's the Cannery. A Sumner icon."

"I've been there," Taryn said, her gaze following where

Bonnie was indicating. "I bought a light oak bedroom set from them. They have some beautiful pieces in the showroom."

"Exactly," said Bonnie, elbowing Taryn gently. Yes, always looking for an excuse to initiate casual contact. She pulled her arm back. "I'll bet they would be proud to host the wedding for Sumner's mayor. And there'd be so many places to sit—just think how much Marty and Lex would save on chair rentals alone. I'll bet they even make a pumpkin fudge in the fall."

"Yeah, too bad we're already locked into a contract with Sumner's iconic cat café. Where, incidentally, there are also plenty of chairs."

"Contracts can be mysteriously ripped to pieces by cats if they're left unattended."

"Which is why the first lesson we learn in Wedding Planner 101 is to always scan and digitally file each document."

"Damn," Bonnie muttered, hiding her smile. She had already agreed to do this, but the occasional hint at an alternative venue wasn't going to hurt.

Taryn settled back in her seat with her elbow resting on the console between them, tantalizingly close to Bonnie's arm. "Quit trying to back out of the deal and tell me more about this farm," she said.

Bonnie sighed in defeat and launched into a description of the farm's herb garden that carried them through the short drive to the Puyallup Valley. She fell silent for the last part of the journey, giving her full attention to the rutted gravel road.

She turned left onto a driveway marked only with a mailbox and a barely readable sign that said *Lee Farm*. They weren't open to the general public most of the year, and all the locals called the place Ben and Daisy's, so they had no need to upgrade their sign. Come September, the road would be graded, and the entire area would be covered with bright and kitschy Halloween decorations—none of Taryn's elegant Halloween here.

"See that bare dirt area?" Bonnie asked, gesturing to her left. "You can see tiny shoots of corn plants. In the fall, it'll be a huge corn maze. That's the pumpkin patch on the other side. The Halloween attractions are here in the front, but the year-long working parts of the farm are behind the house. They also have a few hundred acres in Eastern Washington."

"Wow. That seems like a lot to manage. How many...oh, are those baby goats?"

Bonnie smiled at the delighted expression on Taryn's face. Even people who weren't big animal lovers couldn't seem to resist tiny goats. Bonnie had her suspicions about Taryn and pets, guessing that her stiffness around them was likely more due to lack of exposure than a real dislike.

She parked the car and got out, following Taryn who seemed drawn to the goat pen like a magnet. Bonnie needed to be more careful with the assumptions she made about her. Before long, she might be trying to convince herself that Taryn was someone who really wanted to have a lifestyle that included dozens of cats, but she just hadn't realized it yet. Taryn most likely was quite clear in her mind that she did not want to share in any part of Bonnie's feline-centric lifestyle. Bonnie needed to remember that if she wanted to protect her heart.

She caught up with Taryn and saw Daisy coming out of the main barn, cutting across the yard to meet them. About a decade older than Bonnie, she always managed to look like she was about to go clubbing in a trendy city hotspot, even when she was wearing dirt-smudged overalls and tall rubber boots and holding a fuzzy yellow chick in her gloved hand. If she wore her outfit in Seattle, Bonnie would bet that everyone in the city would be clamoring to match her look, chicken and all. She and her partner Ben had been working in the city when Daisy's parents were killed by a drunk driver. They had quit their jobs, moved to the small town of Puyallup, and taken on the management of an overwhelmingly huge farm. Bonnie admired the way they made it look easy. She knew it was anything but.

Daisy gave her a one-armed hug, and Bonnie introduced her to Taryn.

"Nice to meet you," Daisy said, handing Taryn the chick. "Here's a little welcome-to-the-farm present from me and Ben."

Taryn took the chick with an alarmed look on her face, carefully cupping her free hand over it to keep it from falling. She looked to Bonnie with a help-me expression on her face. "Oh, thank you, but I really couldn't..."

Daisy laughed. "I'm just kidding. It's not really a present." She paused and held out her hand, palm up. "It'll be twenty dollars."

Taryn shook her head and grinned. "I can see why the two of you are friends," she said, gesturing toward Bonnie with her head. "You both share a rather evil sense of humor."

"I might have told her about the rapping cats in their sequined capes," Bonnie admitted as Taryn gently patted the chick on the head with one finger and handed it back to Daisy. "I think this is her version of payback."

"I wish I could have seen the look on her face when you asked her to dress up her cats," Daisy said to Taryn. "You should have filmed her. Now why don't you two go in and see the goats while I give this little one back to his mama."

CHAPTER ELEVEN

Once the threat of becoming a chicken owner was removed, Taryn loved every moment of her time on the farm. She met countless animals, she got to feed some goat kids with a bottle, and Ben gave her a tour of the production areas where they processed honey and goat's milk. He promised to let her put on a beekeeping suit and take a closer look at the hives if she came back.

One of her favorite parts of her job was the opportunity to try new things. Skydiving, hot air ballooning, snowshoeing. She had climbed Mount Rainier and had gotten her scuba certification in order to attend her clients' ceremonies. Even the less adventurous requests, like having the wedding at a brewery or aquarium or museum, often gave her a chance to get interesting glimpses behind the scenes of those familiar places. As a more traditional wedding planner, she would rarely get to experience anything much more exciting than seeing an unfamiliar hotel ballroom or eating yet another plate of dry, roasted chicken with overcooked vegetables.

This current wedding had already led her to some unusual places. Bonnie's café, this farm. She'd love to come back here and see the bees, maybe stop by in the fall for some freshly made cider and to get a pumpkin for her front porch, but she wouldn't want to live here permanently.

That was another good part of her job—she was able to try things, then move on to something new. Just like she'd leave the cat café behind once the wedding was over, maybe stopping by for a coffee and to see Sasha. To say hello to Bonnie.

Of course, on one of those visits, she'd discover that Sasha had been adopted. And Bonnie's new girlfriend would be there, helping behind the counter. They had probably adopted Sasha together and were now living as one big happy family...

"It's an acquired taste," Ben said, breaking her out of her increasingly annoying daydream. "You don't have to eat it if you don't want to."

"No, it's delicious," Taryn said truthfully. Her irritation with Bonnie's imaginary future girlfriend must have shown on her face. She picked up another cracker topped with goat cheese and a drizzle of honey. "I was just trying to figure out what kind of herbs I'm tasting."

Okay, the second part was a lie, but the scenario she had been imagining was much better left unspoken.

"This one has parsley, chives, and tarragon," he said, then continued with the story he had been telling her about when he and Daisy first moved to the farm.

"We had only been living together for two months when it happened," he said, leaning back in his chair and crossing his ankles. They were sitting at a picnic table in front of the main barn waiting for Daisy and Bonnie, who had gone off to harvest something or other—Taryn hadn't really paid attention to what since she'd had five goats trying to drink from her one bottle at the time.

"We hadn't talked much about the future, or where we were heading as a couple. We both had careers that were going great, and it seemed like a perfect time to just be young and free and not care about anything beyond the next weekend's party. Then there was the accident, and I could tell Daisy was going to come back here to the farm no matter what. And I just…well, I just knew I was going with her. Within a month, we quit our jobs and sublet the condo, and here we are."

"Did you have farming experience?" Taryn couldn't imagine changing lifestyles so drastically. She was happy with her habits and her routines, and her job gave her enough variety and challenge to keep things interesting. Would she give it up for another person? Definitely not.

Probably not.

"Zero. Daisy grew up here, so she'd been involved since she was a toddler, but even she had no idea how to actually manage the place. Finances, sales, hiring employees. She had helped with harvests and wore a costume during the pumpkin patch season, but there's so much more to this than she realized. I didn't have any experience at all. Shopping at Pike Place Market was the closest I'd ever come to farm life. We muddled through, though, and we've made it ours. We've added some new crops, and the bees were my special project."

Taryn looked around them. The place was beautiful and peaceful. The garden was full of flowers, and she could see pastures and fields stretching into the distance. These moments of sitting down without hard labor to do must be few and far between, though. "Do you ever regret leaving your old life behind?"

He looked at her with frank brown eyes. "Never. Not even for a second. I expected to, of course. I thought I'd struggle with doubt, maybe even leave if I couldn't handle it, but it was just never an issue. She was here, so I was, too."

He seemed to fit his surroundings, just like Daisy did, but Taryn could just as easily picture both of them in suits in

Seattle, having a power lunch in a fancy waterfront restaurant. His face lit up in a wide smile, and Taryn turned to see Daisy and Bonnie coming around the corner of the barn, both holding large crates stuffed with net bags of produce. Taryn felt her own face stretch in a welcoming smile, but unlike Ben, she tried to keep her expression less noticeable.

Bonnie grinned at her and set the crate on the table, reaching for one of the crackers. "I've got a list of what will be in season in October, plus Daisy had some good ideas for pumpkin dishes. I'll be able to make some of them for Lex and Marty to try Friday."

Bonnie sounded optimistic about the food, but Taryn was still skeptical. "I was thinking we might be able to sell them on a pumpkin-adjacent menu. Meaning we could have some scattered on the buffet table as decoration."

Daisy laughed. "Never underestimate our Bonnie's creativity. She just might surprise you with what she comes up with."

"She definitely is full of surprises," Taryn said with a grin. Daisy raised her eyebrows, possibly reading more into Taryn's comment than she had meant for anyone to notice. Without looking at Bonnie to see if she had registered Taryn's interest in her as well, she continued in a lighter tone. "I'm still expecting her to have a full-blown cat chorus ready to serenade the happy couple."

Her ploy worked, and the four of them spent the next half hour trying to outdo each other with the spectacular cat antics Bonnie could pull off for the wedding. Eventually, they said their good-byes, and Taryn promised to come back to see the bees. As they drove back to the main road, she glanced over the list of October crops Bonnie had handed her.

"Have you looked at these options?" she asked, flipping the page over in case there were tastier-sounding items listed on the back. It was blank. "Rutabagas and cabbage? Brussels sprouts? Are these any good with pumpkin?"

"We'll see. We might have some misses Friday, but we'll figure it out by October."

Taryn shook her head, imagining the look on Marty and Lex's faces when they were served a dish of cabbage mixed with canned pumpkin. "You seem very calm for someone who has to make these ingredients into something we can serve to guests without having them run out of the café and to the nearest McDonald's." She gasped and poked Bonnie in the leg. "This is part of your plan to keep the café from being a dating spot, isn't it? Serve an all-rutabaga menu, and no one will even come in, let alone fall in love."

Bonnie laughed. "It wasn't my plan, but it is now. Thank you." She took Taryn's hand from where it was resting near her leg and gave it a squeeze. "Don't worry. I try new recipes for the café all the time. Some are good, some aren't. You just keep making changes until it works."

Taryn brought her hand slowly back to her lap, trying not to look like she was pulling away from Bonnie's touch. She was pulling away because she liked the feel of Bonnie's hand holding her own far too much.

"*Don't worry.* Easy for you to say. They always blame the wedding planner, no matter what goes wrong. Once word gets out about the Rutabaga Incident, I'll never be hired for another wedding."

"Fine, I'll stick to cabbage if it will make you worry less. Say, Daisy and I found some Lady Fern fiddleheads down by their stream, so I was going to cook them for dinner. Do you want to come home with me and try some?"

Taryn hesitated, and she could feel Bonnie's stillness as she waited for an answer. Was she asking Taryn on a date, or to test out wedding food? Or was this invitation just a casual one Bonnie would extend to any friend? And what the hell was a fiddlehead? Taryn had a fern in her office, and she had never been tempted to chew on it.

"Yes, I'd like that," she said, after realizing she had been silent far too long. No matter what the answers to the questions she had in her mind, her response would have been the same. A date, a tasting, a casual dinner with a friend.

Yes to any or all if it was with Bonnie.

Bonnie nodded as she merged onto the highway. "Good," she said. Her expression didn't give Taryn any clues about what she was feeling, and she steered the conversation back to the rest of the fresh produce she had gotten from the farm while they drove back to Sumner.

Bonnie's house was a narrow two-story tucked on a small lot between two larger ones. The lawn was tidy, but there was little to it beyond the grass and two rhododendrons that flanked the front door. Taryn guessed that most of Bonnie's time and energy was focused on the café, with little left over for gardening here, too. She picked up one of the crates and followed Bonnie into the house with it.

She had expected cats, naturally, but only three came into the living room to curl around Bonnie's legs and welcome her home. Two were mottled black and orange, and one was a tiny striped kitten.

"Do you only have three?" Taryn asked. She set down the crate and scooped up the kitten. She wasn't becoming a Cat Person, but after one look at the fluffy little thing she decided she was more than okay with being a Kitten Person. "I was expecting a houseful."

"Just three," Bonnie confirmed. "These are mine, and the ones at the café are all adoptable. The torties are Frances and Alice, and the kitten is Pepper. He's about three months old."

Taryn reluctantly put Pepper back on the floor and took the crate into the kitchen. She looked around while Bonnie stored the produce away. Just like the outside of the house, the interior was neat, but plain. The cat toys and climbing trees were more adorned than anything that was meant for the human inhabitant.

"I'm eventually planning to move into the café, so this place is just temporary," Bonnie said, correctly guessing what Taryn had been thinking. She paused, then continued with a rueful grin. "Well, it's been temporary since I opened, but I can't take over the upstairs room there until I make another space for the kittens. I have most of my books and stuff upstairs, which is where I spend most of my time when I'm home."

Taryn wandered over to the kitchen table, drawn to the one incongruously cluttered space in the room, and picked up a brochure off the top of a stack. She glanced through it.

"Did you have these made for the adoption event?" she asked. "They're perfect. They cover exactly what we talked about with the different rooms and how to decide what type of cat will fit your lifestyle. How did you...Hey! That cat looks like Sasha."

"It is her," Bonnie said, looking up from where she was standing by the sink, peeling something off a coiled green thing. "Jerome has been taking photos for the website, and I used some to make that brochure after we decided to do the adoption event."

"You made this in just a couple of days?" Taryn skimmed the brochure again, this time recognizing Salmon and Kip and a few other cats, as well as the furnishings in the café. "It looks professionally done. This is impressive work, Bonnie."

Bonnie just shrugged, tossing another green thing into the

pan next to her. "Thanks, but it was easy to throw together. I did marketing for nonprofits, mostly animal rescue groups, for years before I started the café."

"You're kidding me," Taryn said. She pulled out a chair and sat down, and immediately Pepper was next to her, standing on his back legs and stretching as he tried to climb her pant leg. She absently reached down and lifted him onto her lap.

"Nope," Bonnie said. "My parents were thrilled when I finally decided on a major and told them I was studying marketing. They were less enthusiastic when I added the *for nonprofits* part to the career."

Taryn shook her head. This was too much to take in. "When I tried to research your café after Marty hired me, I couldn't find a website or anything on social media. I had to learn about your business from other cat café sites because yours was invisible. And when you get a chance for free publicity practically thrown onto your doorstep, you act like it's the worst thing that's happened to you. Were you any good at your marketing jobs, or were you fired from all of them?"

Bonnie frowned over her shoulder at Taryn as she put the pan on the stove and turned on the heat. "I was very good at them. Mostly."

"Then why aren't you doing the same good work for your own business?"

Taryn could hear her frustration coming through in her voice. She knew she might be crossing a line here, but she honestly didn't understand why Bonnie seemed determined not to support her own café.

She had originally assumed that her nonexistent online presence was due to Bonnie's inexperience with promoting a business, or a lack of skills with technology in general. But she apparently had plenty of skill in graphic design. The brochure was gorgeous with its appealing photos and layout, and its carefully presented information.

"You said you rejected your family's pressure to make a lot of money, but are you seriously trying to make as little as possible just to prove you're not like them? Is it worth sabotaging your business just to prove a point?"

Bonnie stared at her. "I...that's ridiculous. Of course I want the café to do well and make a profit. I've just been too busy to do much marketing. And we've been doing fine without needing to push too hard."

She turned away from Taryn and added some spices to the sizzling pan, sending a burst of mouthwatering scents into the air. Taryn opened the brochure again, careful not to disturb the kitten that was now stretched out on her lap and fast asleep. Bonnie was proving to be much more enigmatic than Taryn had first thought. And much more talented and creative. And stubborn. She wasn't easy to understand, but the more Taryn found out about her, the more she wanted to learn.

At least her idea about the adoption event had encouraged Bonnie to display some of her skills. Hopefully, she wouldn't stop with one brochure.

CHAPTER TWELVE

B onnie took a quiche lorraine out of the fridge and cut two wedges from it, wrapped them in foil, and put them in the oven to reheat.

Sabotaging her own business? As she had already said to Taryn, the notion was ridiculous. She hadn't aggressively promoted the café on social media, but was she actively sabotaging her business?

No, of course not.

She was busy—no one could deny that her days and evenings were full. She had the occasional time off, like her Sundays, but even those were often spent caring for the animals or shopping for supplies.

When did Taryn expect her to work on this grand marketing plan? From two to three in the morning? While she was stirring muffin batter?

Well, she had managed to get the brochure done while eating a sandwich in the café, before the lunch crowds arrived. Between her own photos and Jerome's, she now had a huge selection on her laptop. She had known exactly what she wanted to say because the lecture she often gave about choosing a new pet was always clear in her mind after so many years of delivering it to potential adopters.

It had taken maybe half an hour to combine the pictures and text into a cohesive package and then email the file to an office supply store on South Hill, requesting expedited printing. Another fifteen minutes to pick up the finished product while running other errands. No one could argue that her life wasn't hectic at times and always full, but she'd have a hard time convincing even herself that she couldn't find a spare forty-five minutes in a day.

She glanced over and saw Taryn still reading through the damned brochure. She peered over the edge of it every few seconds, though, so Bonnie didn't think she was actually absorbing the material. More likely, she was giving Bonnie time to mull over what she had said. Or waiting for her to explode in anger and kick Taryn out of the house for prying into her life.

The latter did tempt her, only because it would let Bonnie off the hook and she could continue on her way, remaining in denial over the accuracy of Taryn's statements.

But Bonnie didn't want her to go. She enjoyed Taryn's company, for one thing, as brief as their acquaintance was destined to be. For another, she felt an edge of truth to what Taryn had told her. She didn't think anyone else in her life would have been as blunt about it.

Jerome had scolded her about not having a website, but he seemed to assume that she had quit developing one because she didn't know how. Nancy's main concerns would be that Bonnie stayed in business, no matter how slim her profit margins, and that she continued to be a pushover when Nancy had another cat to add to her menagerie. Viv would give Taryn a run for her money in candor, but her focus was on Bonnie's love life and not the café's solvency. And Isa—well, since she was working with Bonnie on managing the café's books, she'd probably soon be coming after her to be more proactive with marketing. For all Isa's talk about a business's worth being measured in more than just financial terms, she had a distinctly practical side to her and probably wouldn't be quiet about it.

Bonnie filled bowls of food for the cats while dinner finished cooking. She was relieved when the two torties merely wound around her legs in anticipation rather than hopping onto the counter as they often did. Taryn would never believe she didn't have cats climbing all over her café's kitchen counters if she saw it happening right in front of her eyes in Bonnie's home.

She put the bowls down near the back door and went over to Taryn to get Pepper. He had woken up and was batting at a frayed thread on Taryn's sweatshirt sleeve, which was very cute, but unless he was put right by his food, the others would eat it. She reached down to pick him up, which necessitated far more contact with Taryn's inner thighs than she had anticipated. She made herself stand up and exhale slowly to keep from leaping away from Taryn with an audible gasp. Touching her was always far more electrically charged than should be expected from casual contact, and the intimacy of being practically in Taryn's lap only intensified the sensation.

"He needs to eat his dinner," she said, surprised to hear her voice sounding calm and not squeaky. She put him next to his bowl and returned to stand by Taryn—although not nearly as close this time.

"I think you might have a somewhat valid point," she said. "I might have reasons why I'm…well, hesitant when it comes to heavily marketing my business, but I promise I'm trying to deal with them. I'd never want to jeopardize the café, or especially the chance to get more cats into forever homes, because of them. I shouldn't have gotten so defensive when you were only trying to help."

"Hey, I get it," Taryn said. She stood up and reached toward Bonnie's arm, pulling her hand back before she made contact. "The choices we make with our businesses aren't always logical and disconnected from our lives. You were partly right about why I plan the kinds of weddings I do. In some ways, it's a reaction to my childhood. I do this because I hope that if two people come together in an honest way, being true to themselves even if the ceremony they choose isn't what anyone else would want, then their marriage has to stand a better chance than if they're just following customs that have nothing to do with them personally. It doesn't always work, but I feel I've done something to help."

When Taryn paused, Bonnie took her hand and pulled her away from the table and over to the kitchen island. "Keep talking," she said softly, not wanting to break the spell of Taryn's words, and not just because she was relieved to have the conversation's focus turned away from her. She wanted to learn more about Taryn for purely personal reasons.

She let go of Taryn's hand and put on an oven mitt to get the quiche out of the oven before it burned. It was an extremely poor substitute for the feel of Taryn's skin against her own.

"You should see the photos from my parents' wedding," Taryn continued, resting her hip against the island. "It was gorgeous, from her dress to these amazing floral displays to the stained glass in the church. Really stunning. I used to sneak into their room and look through the album when I was home by myself. They looked so happy, and I wanted so badly to make them feel that way again. I felt like I could make it happen, and if it didn't, then it was because I wasn't trying hard enough. But as I got older, I realized they didn't look like themselves in those pictures. They were dressed up, made-up, and told when to smile. That's when I knew that nothing I did was going to change the way they were. The happiness I saw in the album was false, so there wasn't anything to recapture. It had never existed in the first place."

Bonnie scooped some fiddleheads out of the sauté pan and onto the plates next to the quiche. She hadn't heard Taryn talk this much about herself since they had met—actually, she said very little about herself unless prompted. She wanted to reassure Taryn that she hadn't failed her parents, and that no child should ever be responsible for repairing their parents' relationship, but she remained quiet, not wanting to interrupt. Besides, Taryn knew those things. She wasn't a child anymore. Bonnie thought maybe it was more healing for her to be able to talk freely about her past than for her to hear platitudes and reassurances that she no longer needed as an adult.

"Oh, those are fiddleheads," Taryn said, switching out of storytelling mode and focusing on their dinner. "I've seen pictures of them, but I've never tried one. How do they taste? Because they smell divine."

"They taste…green. And earthy. The smell is from the spices, and they help balance some of the bitterness of the fronds," Bonnie said, accepting the change in topic without protest.

Taryn would talk more about her past when she wanted to. Or she wouldn't. Bonnie was grateful for everything she learned about her but understood the need for a break. "It's one of my own blends, made of savory, marjoram, thyme, nutmeg, cinnamon, and cloves. You won't find fiddleheads in October, but I thought the spice blend would be good in one of the pumpkin dishes. I'm sure it will go really well with rutabagas."

"What doesn't?" Taryn asked sarcastically. She followed Bonnie back to the table and sat down across from her. "Thank you for this. I get takeout far too often, and it's been a while since I've had a homecooked meal."

"Café-cooked," Bonnie said. "I have to do so much baking there that I usually just make an extra of the special of the day and bring it home."

"Hmm," Taryn said, lifting her plate and inspecting the quiche. "Did Kip help you make this?"

"Of course not. Well, he might have observed the process, but from all the way across the room. He kept all his fur over there with him."

Taryn laughed and took a small, experimental bite of a fiddlehead frond. "Ooh, I like this. It's crunchier than I expected."

Their conversation over dinner remained neutral and unencumbered by their pasts. They talked about food and cooking, and when Bonnie's cats finished their dinners and wandered back to the table, Bonnie told Taryn about how she had come to adopt her three.

"Frances and Alice are sisters. I fostered the litter for my friend Nancy. She's the one who brought me Salmon, as well as about half of my other cats."

"Ah, Ninja Cat. Now I know who is to blame if he chews off any of the guests' limbs at the wedding."

"He's all glare and no bite," Bonnie assured her. "Just be careful not to try to touch him. Or make direct eye contact. And whatever you do, don't show any fear."

"I'll be sure to put that warning on the wedding invitations. Go on, then. Did you adopt the entire litter?"

"No, just the two. It's a common rookie mistake, and part of the reason why foster homes are so scarce. If you keep adopting them, you eventually have to stop fostering because you don't have the time or money or space to take care of your own animals, let alone bring home more."

"So you have to keep yourself from getting attached?"

"Not at all. I get emotional every time one of my café cats

is adopted." Bonnie hesitated, then admitted the truth. "Okay, I cry like a baby each time because I love them and will miss them, but it's more a way of recognizing how wonderful each cat is than mourning a loss. Adoption days are the best days, even if they make me sad. Adoptions are the goal. A cat gets its own home and family, and I have space so I can give another rescue cat a chance at the same thing."

"It's amazing, what you do," Taryn said. She leaned over and picked up Pepper, who was trying to climb her pant leg again. "Although that makes me wonder how you ended up with this little one. He was just too cute to pass up, yes he was."

"Did you just talk baby talk to a kitten?" Bonnie asked.

This side of Taryn was one she hadn't seen before. Maybe all this time around Bonnie's cats was making Taryn…She caught herself before she finished the thought. Tiny, fluffy Pepper was a darling. Anyone would fall in love with him, and she had better remember that snuggling one little kitten did not mean someone was turning into an *I really think we need two dozen of these* cat fanatic.

"I do not talk baby talk to anyone, human or animal," Taryn said with an indignant scowl. It might have been a more effective expression if she didn't have Pepper tucked between her chin and shoulder. "And you'd better not tell anyone I did, especially my assistant Angie. I have an icy reputation to maintain."

Bonnie smiled. *Icy* wasn't the word she'd use to describe Taryn. Hot was more like it. Fiery, passionate, and fierce. There was nothing cold about her.

"Pepper sort of found me," Bonnie explained, trying to stop her rampant thoughts about Taryn. "He was in the backyard one day, mewing and alone. I put up signs and asked my neighbors, but either no one belonged to him, or they didn't want to admit it. I couldn't find a mother cat or the rest of the litter, so I assumed he was dumped around here and just wandered into my yard. He was too young for the kitten room at the café, and I have plenty of room for three."

Bonnie stood up and stacked their empty plates. Taryn was watching her, and Bonnie could see the moment when her expression grew serious again.

"Back to our earlier conversation," she said, cradling Pepper in her arms. "I have a theory about why subconsciously you might not want the café to turn into a really profitable business—if you don't mind me meddling a bit?"

Bonnie paused as she was putting the plates in the dishwasher. She raised her eyebrows at Taryn.

Taryn laughed unselfconsciously. "Okay, I've already meddled, so it's a little late to be asking permission, but I really will shut up and stop intruding if you ask me to."

Bonnie waved her on. "Go ahead. Analyze me."

"It's just…I agree with what you said about my career when you were at the office, about why I chose this path. And everything I said earlier is true. But there's another reason, and it's more about stubbornness than pain. I think I wanted to prove a point. To essentially say with my decision that I think my parents were wrong. Marriages and relationships don't have to be spiteful or miserable. They can be wonderful and empowering and healthy. I don't know if I fully believe it on a personal level, since I've never experienced it, but with every wedding I plan, I affirm that I hope it's true."

Taryn paused, and Bonnie desperately wanted to fill the space and keep the conversation focused on her, not letting it turn back to Bonnie and the café.

Or change the subject back to cats.

She was fine talking about cats. Talking about herself and her issues? No.

But still, she kept silent and waited for Taryn to finish making her point.

"I wholeheartedly believe you have devoted your life to your café because you care about the animals and about doing your part to get these lonely strays into homes. It's beautiful, Bonnie, it really is. And it's admirable the way you defied what you were taught to want and instead made a life based on your own values. But I wonder if there's a part of you that is stubbornly trying to make the point that money doesn't have as much meaning for you as it does for your family. If your café becomes a success and you open franchises across the country, making millions of dollars of profit every year, you sort of lose your moral high ground, don't you."

"I...um..." Bonnie struggled to find a way to respond. "But I made those brochures. We're going to have a website, and I said yes to the wedding. I'm making an effort."

"Meh. You agreed to the wedding because you're kind, and you know how much your café means to Marty and Lex. You made the brochure and will probably make every effort to turn Finding Furever into a spectacular event because there are other rescue groups involved, and they're friends of yours. Would you do the same if any of this was just for you and your café?"

Not a chance.

Bonnie admitted it to herself but refused to say it out loud. Not that she needed to—Taryn's smug expression showed that she knew exactly what Bonnie was thinking.

"Just do me a favor sometime, once you've thought about this," Taryn said. "Pretend you're back in your marketing days, and you've been hired to promote this small-town cat café. Look at it from an outsider's perspective, knowing that the more successful they are, the more cats they'll be able to rescue."

"Yes, I'll give it a try," Bonnie said. Sometime.

Still, it was a reasonable request, and agreeing would likely end this part of the conversation. Even if Taryn's theory helped in part to explain her behavior, Bonnie didn't need to fill in the rest of the equation for her. Hopefully, this little chat would be enough to assuage Taryn's interest in Bonnie's actions and would keep her from doing any Google searches in an effort to learn more.

With the fluidity that Bonnie was coming to expect from her time with Taryn, their conversation turned easily back to casual territory—some of Taryn's funniest wedding mishaps— as Bonnie drove them back through the quiet, dark streets to the café. They said good-bye on the sidewalk, and then Bonnie let herself into the café to check on the cats. She was tempted to ask Taryn to join her, but the empty café seemed too close and intimate. Their conversations had crossed far beyond surface talk tonight, and Bonnie wasn't yet ready for more.

Until Taryn had driven away, and she was sitting alone on the floor, visiting with the animals and wishing Taryn was still with her.

Eventually she sighed and stood up, letting Kip follow her into the kitchen. She might as well start planning Friday's all-pumpkin tasting menu.

CHAPTER THIRTEEN

On Friday, Taryn held open the door to Bonnie's cat café and let Marty and Lex enter first. She was just being polite and was absolutely not using them as a shield in case Bonnie came at her, angry about Taryn's interference in her business and personal life.

They hadn't spoken to each other since Wednesday, but it wasn't as if they had any reason to interact unless they were working together on plans for the wedding or the adoption event. And it had only been one day. Somehow, though, Taryn had felt the lack of Bonnie with the same disconcerting feeling she might have had if she walked into the office and her desk was gone, or Angie wasn't there, like a familiar piece of her life was missing.

Maybe Taryn was the one who should be angry. Bonnie had no right to become an integral part of Taryn's life. They might fit together really well when they were sharing dinner or talking about…well, about anything…but Bonnie came as a package deal, and Taryn's world didn't have room for a house full of cats. Two houses, actually, although the second one had a more manageable number of felines. Even three were more than Taryn needed in her life.

Still, she had spent yesterday worried that she had messed things up with Bonnie by being far too pushy and intrusive.

It would make her sad if Bonnie grew more distant with her because of it, but Taryn knew deep inside that it was worth her losing their growing friendship if it meant Bonnie eventually took her comments to heart and made some changes in the café. She was doing wonderful work here, and she could do so much more if she stopped undermining herself and limiting the café's potential.

Taryn had a feeling that a Bonnie unfettered by her past would be an unstoppable force. She had a strength to her that Taryn hadn't fully appreciated until they talked at dinner. She had taken on a job that intentionally—and even *hopefully*—was full of good-byes and heartache. Even Taryn, who wasn't an animal lover—well, except for Pepper because he was too cute for words, and sweet Sasha, and maybe even poor misunderstood Ninja Cat—would have a hard time letting go of beloved animals day after day, week after week. Taryn easily said good-bye to her clients after their weddings, but they usually kept in touch, and it wasn't as if she had lived with them and cared for them for months.

Thank goodness.

Taryn followed Lex and Marty through the second door. She looked around in surprise at the way the café seemed transformed from what she had seen the other times she had come.

Her previous visits had been in the late morning, between breakfast and lunch, and only a few patrons had been at the tables. Now, almost all of them were full, and customers were scattered on cushions on the floor, as well. The cats seemed to be responding to the increased activity, and most of them were leaping around, chasing after cat toys on strings. Others were sunning themselves on perches by the windows or in laps of coffee drinkers.

"Wow," Taryn said. "It was pretty quiet when I was here before, but this is amazing."

"Cat cafés are a brilliant concept," Lex agreed. "It's similar to staging a house, like we do in real estate when we want homebuyers to be able to picture themselves living there, more than they would if they were just looking at blank walls and bare floors. In this case, instead of walking through a depressing concrete facility with animals in cages, you get to see them interacting in an environment that is similar to your own home."

"Plus, people know the cats are cared for and have a good life here," Bonnie said from behind Taryn. "Not as great as a forever home, but one that is safe and interesting and fun."

Taryn spun around at the sound of Bonnie's voice. She was wearing a jacket and holding a cat carrier and must have followed them into the café.

"That makes the experience more relaxing," Bonnie continued. "In a shelter, some people just rush through and then leave because the environment is too emotionally stressful for them. Others panic at the thought of a cat being put to sleep and adopt too quickly, possibly regretting it later if the animal isn't a good fit for their household."

She paused and gave Marty and Lex each a kiss on the cheek in greeting. When she came to Taryn, she seemed unsure about what to do, and after a moment of hesitation, switched the carrier to her left hand and reached out to shake Taryn's.

Taryn hid her grin as well as she could. Bonnie seemed awkward, not angry, which was fine. Taryn felt a little awkward around her, too.

"Is the cat all right?" she asked, pointing at the carrier. She could only see some tufts of gray fur where the cat was pressed against the wire mesh door.

"Yes. This is Tulip. I just picked her up from the vet. She had a dental cleaning and is still a little groggy from the anesthetic, so I'm going to shut her in the upstairs room so she can have some peace and quiet while she sleeps it off. I reserved the table in the back for you, so go ahead and have a seat, and I'll be right back with some dishes to try."

Taryn held back and let them start walking toward the table before leaning closer to Bonnie. "Did you look out a window and name her after the first thing you saw?"

"No," Bonnie said indignantly, but then she smiled. "Well, yes. She was lucky I looked out the side window and not the back, or she'd be named Dumpster."

Bonnie winked at her and headed upstairs, leaving Taryn with a smile on her face and Marty and Lex watching her from the table. She tried to look like she was smiling at all the adorable cats but doubted she pulled it off.

"It's so much fun to watch the cats playing," she said when she sat down. Bonnie had pushed two tables together in the back, where Taryn had sat before, and put a delicately hand-lettered *Reserved* sign on it.

They just laughed at her. "It sure is," Marty said as he and Lex shared the same look every couple did when they thought they were witnessing someone in love, as if they were telepathically saying *Aw, she's one of us now.* Taryn had no intention of joining the we're-in-love tribe.

She was about to steer the conversation back where it belonged—to their wedding and not anywhere near her personal life—when Sasha jumped in her lap. Great. Now she not only had a usual table in a cat café, but her lap had become the usual seat for one of the cats. She tried to remain indifferent to the now-familiar weight of the cat and her ridiculously deep purr, but she felt a weird sort of pride. Last time she was here, she had been Sasha's only option for a human chair. Today the cat had an abundance of choice, but here she was.

She cleared her throat and started talking about the schematics of the ceremony, and luckily the topic was met with enthusiasm as the three of them discussed where to put the altar they were planning to create and how to arrange the tables.

She could handle this. Bonnie, Sasha—they were minor distractions, but when she put her mind to her job, everything else faded into the background.

She barely noticed Bonnie walking past them in those jeans that made Taryn want to follow her into the kitchen, lock the door, and rip them off...

Okay, maybe she needed to aim for reasonably competent instead of highly focused. Even that was a stretch, though, when Bonnie came over with a plate with four tiny tartlets on it and reached past Taryn to put it in the center of the table. She smelled like she had been rolling in baked goods. Damn.

"You can start with this while I get the rest," Bonnie said. "Phyllo cups with spiced kale, chard, pumpkin, and feta. Of course, all the greens and pumpkin will be in season for the wedding, so they'll be fresh and more flavorful than these. I'll use rainbow chard then, but I could only find Swiss now, and it's tougher than what I'll get from the farm. The pumpkin is frozen, so the texture isn't perfect, but—"

Marty held up his hand. "Would you please shut up so we can eat this? It smells heavenly."

Bonnie laughed and returned to the kitchen. She had barely taken a step away from the table when the three of them reached out and each grabbed an appetizer.

Taryn had seen both kale and chard on the list Bonnie had gotten from the farm, and she had thought they sounded rather unpleasant. She had been oh so wrong. The spice blend had to be the same one Bonnie had used on the fiddleheads, and it tasted even better combined with the salty, creamy feta and the slightly sweet pumpkin.

They were silent while they ate, except for some mumbled *mmm*s. Taryn looked at the last tart, wondering how unprofessional it would be to take it instead of letting one of her clients have it.

"If you eat that, you're fired," Marty said.

"Oh yeah? If you eat it, I'm adopting every one of those kittens, and you'll have an empty dressing room."

"Oh, good," Bonnie said. She was back at the table and holding two more plates. "I have plenty more in the kitchen, but I wanted to find out what you really thought of them."

"You only gave us four on purpose?" Lex asked in disbelief. "What is this, some cat café version of a horror movie?"

Bonnie laughed. "No, I would have stopped you before anyone got violent. I figured if you thought they were bad or just okay, you'd try to get someone else to eat the last one. Since you were fighting for it, you must have liked them."

"I loved *them*," Lex said. "You, I'm not so sure about."

Marty shook his head at Taryn. "She turned us against each other when it's really her we should be after."

"Are you kidding," Taryn hissed in a loud whisper. "She's the one with the food. At least be nice to her until we get the recipe."

Bonnie tapped her forehead. "It's all in here, and none of you are getting any of the recipes." She set two more plates on the table. "Now try these. The pastries are filled with mushrooms, thyme, leeks, and pumpkin. And this is lentil and pumpkin stew with carrots and potatoes. I thought we could serve it in hollowed-out gourds—the little colorful ones people use for decorating at Thanksgiving. I'll be right back with dessert."

They dug in, and after a few bites, Taryn decided pumpkin was her new favorite food. How had she not realized what a perfect idea it was to have an all-pumpkin wedding menu?

Bonnie joined them for her dessert offering, which was a pumpkin-swirl cheesecake topped with a cinnamon apple compote.

"I can change anything you want," Bonnie said, setting her fork on her empty plate. "And I'll come up with more options, too."

Marty took another bite of stew and then gestured with his spoon toward the table. "Add anything you want. Do not take any of these off the menu. I'm going to go visit the cats now, but I might accidentally end up in the kitchen where you said you had more of those tartlets hidden."

"Help yourself," Bonnie said. She licked the last crumbs of cheesecake off her fork, then glanced down and pointed at the ground next to Taryn. "Oh, look."

Taryn, distracted by the sight of Bonnie's tongue, looked absently in the direction Bonnie had indicated. Ninja Cat was sitting on the floor next to her foot, less than a centimeter from touching her shoe. She didn't honestly think he was going to attack her, but the sight of him so stealthily close made her startle. Which upset Sasha.

"Ow." Taryn gasped as four sets of claws dug into her thighs. She tried to pick Sasha up, but she seemed to have become attached to Taryn's flesh.

"Oh, she's stuck. Let me help." Bonnie stood up and reached for the little cat, carefully rotating her paws enough to remove the tiny fishhooks from Taryn's skin. She would probably have felt more pain if she hadn't been overly aware of Bonnie's hands in her lap.

Again.

She kept putting them there, but not doing anything productive with them other than removing cats.

"Well, that hurt," Taryn said. "Hey, give her back."

Bonnie was about to walk away with Sasha, but she paused. "I thought you wanted her off."

"I didn't want her gone—I just didn't want her embedded in me," Taryn said, reaching to take the cat out of Bonnie's arms, which just seemed to tangle the two of them together.

"Careful," Lex said. "You know how easy it is to fall in love here."

"Just because we're spending time together does not mean we are in love," Taryn said sternly, settling Sasha down on her lap again. Salmon hadn't budged, even with all the commotion. "All right, we had one meal together, but the only reason we did was because we were at the farm researching food for your wedding."

"Exactly. It was more a business meeting than a meal," Bonnie said. "And it's not any easier to fall in love here than anywhere else," she added in an exasperated tone.

"Er, I think they were talking to me," Marty said. He was standing near the table holding Kip.

Lex smirked. "I was. I was warning Marty because we don't need another cat. I have no idea what's up with the two of you."

Taryn took a deep breath and exhaled slowly. "That's exactly what I meant." She gestured around the table at the remains of their appetizers. "Just because you share some food here does not mean you have to adopt a cat."

"Yes, that's what I meant, too," Bonnie said in a haughty tone. "That it's no easier to fall in love *with a cat* here than anywhere else." She looked around the room. "Well, there are a lot of them, so I suppose the odds are slightly higher."

Marty and Lex exchanged another amused look as Bonnie disappeared swiftly into the kitchen and Taryn gathered Sasha into her arms and stood up. "I should get going," she said, gently placing Sasha on a nearby cat tree. "This has been…"

"Amusing?" offered Lex.

"Really funny," Marty said.

Bonnie came out of the kitchen with a stack of pastry boxes tied with ribbons. "Leftovers," she said briefly, handing one to each of them. "I'm going upstairs to check on Tulip."

They said a chorus of good-byes—two edged with laughter and two without. Marty and Lex headed out, and Taryn lagged behind for just a moment. She leaned down and gave Salmon a quick pat, which he didn't seem to mind at all, and prepared to go as well—with only one glance toward the staircase where she had last seen Bonnie and only one or two moments of temptation to follow her.

She shook it off, though, and walked out of the café, leaving the cats and Bonnie behind.

CHAPTER FOURTEEN

I t was the most humiliating experience."
Bonnie took a bite of her chicken enchilada and chewed slowly, replaying the end of Friday's tasting in her mind. "They were talking about adopting cats, and Taryn and I just started jabbering about not being in love, like two guilty teenagers who were caught making out." She frowned, not sure whether she was more upset by the misunderstanding or by Taryn's almost frantic denial of having feelings for Bonnie.

"She really didn't have to sound so horrified by the idea."

Viv chuckled, spooning some roasted vegetables into a tortilla and topping them with salsa. "And how did you sound?"

"Horrified," Bonnie admitted. "But not because she's repulsive or anything, just because I desperately wanted them to understand that we're not in love."

"See, when you say it in such a shrill way, all I hear is that you're desperately in love with her."

"I am not," Bonnie growled.

Viv laughed. "Okay, now I believe you. So is this why we're eating here today instead of in Sumner? Not that I'm complaining. The food is delicious."

"We've talked about coming here plenty of times," Bonnie said, which was true. The locally owned Mexican restaurant had a buffet lunch on Sundays and was often on their list of potential restaurants for their meals together, even though they rarely ate anywhere but their favorite place.

"Yes, we've talked about it, but you always say you don't want to drive all the way up here to Auburn."

"Oh, fine. I didn't want to risk running into Marty or Lex. I'm currently avoiding all of Sumner except for my café, and yesterday I stayed in the kitchen most of the day."

And she had hidden upstairs on Friday until she was sure the two of them and Taryn had left.

Sitting next to a drowsy Tulip, she had gone over the embarrassing scene in her mind, wondering why a simple misunderstanding that should have been funny had made her react so emphatically. Well, she knew why, but she hated admitting it even to herself. She had panicked at the thought of anyone—especially Taryn—figuring out that her attraction to and interest in Taryn had grown into something deeper, without her even being aware it was happening until forced to face it by Lex's inadvertent comment.

It wasn't love, not yet, but Taryn was beginning to matter to her, and Bonnie was going to get hurt if she didn't get control over her feelings pretty damned soon.

"This Taryn seems to have gotten under your skin. Do you think dating her might lead to something?"

Bonnie choked on the tortilla chip she was eating and had to take a drink of water to stop coughing. "We're not dating. That was the whole point of my story—that we wanted everyone to know we're not dating."

"Didn't you have dinner with her at your house? And you went to the farm together?"

"We went to the farm because we were exploring options for the wedding food," Bonnie explained, intentionally keeping her voice pitched low. She really didn't believe she was shrill when she talked about Taryn, but she didn't want to take a chance of letting her feelings slip through in her voice. "And after that business trip, we ate some of the produce we bought as a taste test."

"A private taste test just two days before the actual tasting with the couple."

"Yes." Bonnie didn't mention that the produce they tasted had an extremely short harvesting season and would be a mere memory come October.

"So, you call the two of us having brunch a date, but when you take a drive out to the country with an eligible woman to whom you're obviously attracted, and then you take her to your house and cook dinner for her, you're determined not to call it a date?"

Well, when she put it that way, it sounded romantic. Which it hadn't been.

Bonnie was glad she had carefully omitted the part where she had her hands in Taryn's lap when she had recounted the story to Viv.

"It was leftover quiche. I just heated it up."

"Oh, leftover quiche. Why didn't you say so? Then obviously it wasn't a date. I thought you maybe had filet mignon for two, followed by chocolate-covered strawberries and whipped cream. *Then* it would have been a date."

Viv rolled her eyes, as if her sarcastic tone wasn't enough to get her point across, and took another tortilla out of the clay dish.

Bonnie wrestled with the two options of changing the subject entirely or asking Viv about something she'd had on her mind since her evening with Taryn. The need to figure herself out won.

"She did say something that got me thinking about the café and how much effort I put into it."

Viv put down her fajita. "Are you kidding? Did she say you don't work hard enough? Because I've never known anyone who put as much time and love into an endeavor as you have in your café." She reached into her bag and pulled out her phone. "What's her number? We need to have a little chat."

"She didn't call me lazy, so put your phone away," Bonnie said with a laugh. "But thank you for leaping to my rescue. She wasn't talking about what I do there, with all the baking and taking care of the cats. She meant the way I treat the business. She thinks I'm sabotaging its chances to make much money."

"Do you make much money?"

"No. Enough to get by, though." Barely, some months. And unexpected vet bills or unplanned appliance repairs usually managed to wipe out the occasional higher-than-usual profits. "Taryn thinks it's because of my parents. I didn't tell her the real reason why I don't want to push for more publicity."

"Oh, she believes you're trying to be unsuccessful just to prove you're not them? I guess that does make sense. They believe it's important to make a lot of money, so you're determined not to. That might be why you're holding on to past embarrassments and using them as a shield."

Bonnie shook her head firmly. "It's a simple matter of not wanting that damned GIF to go viral again. It has nothing to do with my parents."

Viv shrugged. "The reasons behind our actions are never as simple as we like to think. I'm surprised to hear about all this, though. I assumed your café was doing well because I saw what you did for those nonprofits you worked for after college—not counting the last one, of course. I know the first two you worked for were about to close their doors when you stepped in and turned them around. They're still going strong today because of you. I figured if you were such a success at marketing other people's ventures, you'd work miracles for a business you personally owned, especially since you weren't putting any effort into your love life and had all that energy to spare. I guess it's been the opposite, then?"

Bonnie stayed silent, staring at her plate and picking her fork through a pile of guacamole.

She really had done a great job for those nonprofits. All of them, even that damned last one. She wasn't always comfortable bragging about her own achievements, but in these cases, she had made a difference in a very measurable way through her aggressive marketing and her relentless brainstorming sessions with the staffs as they searched for unconventional opportunities for income, as well as more traditional ones like grants that the groups weren't taking advantage of to the extent she thought they should.

They had been failing, and she not only saved them but helped them thrive.

When she had opened her café, it hadn't even occurred to her to apply the same rigorous approach to the management of her own business. She couldn't explain why without at least partially including Taryn's reasoning.

"You do realize that you're missing the other half of the equation, don't you?" Viv asked gently.

"What do you mean?"

"You always put the two concepts together, but now you're not. You always phrase it in some variation of how your parents wanted you to get married and have a lot of children or get a job that made a lot of money. You repeat it often."

Bonnie wanted to claim that she rarely said those words or any similar ones, but she couldn't deny that Viv was merely repeating a familiar refrain of hers. "Well, I heard it often enough when I was growing up."

"I know. Those two things are always linked in your mind.

And now you're recognizing that you might not be living up to your café's full earning potential because you haven't put your heart into it. But you also need to consider that you aren't putting your heart into finding love, either. Not the marriage and huge family kind of love your parents expected, but a partnership that's right for you."

"I told you. I don't date because once people who don't know me well find that GIF, that's all they see when they look at me."

"Simple as that, hmm? Maybe it's time to let all those reasons go and take a chance on the future instead of the past."

Bonnie propped her elbow on the table and rested her chin on her hand. This was getting exhausting. She was thinking more along the lines of making a few changes to the way she managed her business, not overhauling her whole life.

"Self-reflection sucks," she said.

Viv reached across the table and patted her on the head. "I know, sweetie. Trouble is, once you start, it's impossible to go back to ignoring what you've learned. Just don't rush into anything, and you'll be fine."

Bonnie could do without the head-patting, but the advice was sound.

She'd start with the adoption event. As Taryn had observed, Bonnie was perfectly comfortable putting her full effort into making the event a success because it would benefit Nancy and the other rescue groups involved. Then she'd slowly look for ways to get her café onto the more comfortable side of the bottom line.

As for love...she wasn't sure what to do about that. *Doing nothing* sounded appealing. She didn't know what a love that was just right for her would even look like.

She picked up the chili pepper garnish from their plate of nachos and took a bite, letting the searing heat in her mouth drive away the image of Taryn that had just come unbidden to her mind.

❖

For the next few days, Bonnie threw herself into preparing for the event. She and Taryn talked on the phone a few times, but each time Taryn called, she had a specific question to ask and didn't spend much time on small talk once it had been answered.

Their relationship turned virtual, which was even less date-like than reheated quiche. Taryn sent photos of the venue—Sumner's new community rec center near Loyalty Park, the construction of which had been one of the cornerstones of Marty's campaign. Bonnie visited the center with Marty and texted Taryn with her thoughts about the themes for each room. Taryn was in charge of ticket sales and deposited money into Bonnie's account for buying ingredients and decorations, while Bonnie emailed the images of her menu and the order of serving each dish.

They might as well have been planning the event from opposite sides of the globe and not a mere ten minutes apart for all they saw each other.

And Bonnie missed her.

Not that she had much time to spend thinking about Taryn, though, with the adoption event looming ever closer. Bonnie wasn't bringing many of her own cats, which should have made her life easier, but instead had the opposite effect. She not only had to set up the space for the cats from the three participating groups, but she also had to make sure her café had a strong presence at the event, even without many of its residents in attendance.

She had made a display using blown-up versions of

Jerome's photos, and she was using the rec center's large screens to project the café's two webcams in the reception area. She hadn't wanted to expose the kittens to so much unaccustomed activity—and besides, most of this batch of babies were already spoken for, and they'd soon be going to forever homes or filtering in with the other café cats, to be replaced by more of Nancy's orphaned litters—but at least everyone would be able to watch them play.

Jonah had happily agreed to bring her two young nieces to sit in the room and have a staged children's tea party with the kittens. She and Jerome had carefully planned how their little party would be arranged, so the cameras would capture it to the best effect. She had to admit, the final result was likely to be cringingly cute. Her PR self figured she'd be booked out for at least the next six months of Kitten and Cream Teas after this.

Nancy and the other two rescue groups were thrilled with the opportunity and had sent her detailed lists of all their cats along with current vet certificates, recommending which of the rooms would best suit each one and adding personal notes about how sweet or wonderful or has-some-special-needs-but-is-very-loving every single one of them was.

Trying to shuffle the feline adoption prospects into a safe configuration was proving to be an almighty headache of a chore. She did her best to keep cats that were familiar with each other together, and she was using every ounce of space in the rec center to keep from overcrowding any one room. She felt as if she was planning a wedding reception seating chart for a family full of divorces and feuding relatives.

It was worth every ounce of the stress it caused, though. These groups didn't have the consistent public exposure her café did, so the chance to get their cats seen by a horde of visitors was a real gift to them. There was already talk of having her organize this as an annual event, so maybe it was a good thing Taryn wasn't coming within kicking distance these days.

But she'd better not let Taryn or Viv hear her complaining about the amount of work this was taking or her wariness about committing to doing this all over again next year and the next. The ticket sales were generating far more cash than she had expected, which was likely because Taryn had taken charge of setting prices and advertising the event. Bonnie was able to focus on decorations and food and scheduling.

Which had brought her to a nearby pet store with plenty of money to spend, which was a welcome change from her usual visits.

Taking her cue from the wedding decorations for Marty and Lex, she was using new beds and toys to adorn the rooms instead of adding irrelevant frills. She had considered variations on some elaborate themes but had finally settled on simply assigning each room its own color. Cat paraphernalia and human place settings would match, which made it easy for her to color-code information about specific cats and each room's general type of feline in the information packets each guest would receive.

Bonnie pushed her cart toward the cat section of the store but stopped next to several large clearance bins full of Valentine's Day toys and plushies. A lot of them were meant for dogs but would still brighten the room. And one of the groups participating also rescued dogs, so they'd be able to put the toys to good use after the event.

Bonnie sighed and stopped trying to convince herself when she already knew what she had to do. She emptied the bins into her cart and continued toward the nonseasonal merchandise.

She wasn't sure how she had come to this—running a massive adoption event, planning a wedding in her café, getting back to her old ways of designing marketing material.

And now, pushing a cart full of heart-shaped toys and little cupid plushies through the pet store.

Jerome was going to have hysterics when he saw this.

Bonnie blamed Taryn for all of it.

CHAPTER FIFTEEN

In the days after the tasting, Taryn tried her best to keep its embarrassing details from Angie.

She would have succeeded, too, because she definitely did not want to talk about it, and she had absolutely no trouble keeping herself quiet on the topic. Unfortunately, she hadn't counted on Marty showing up at her office to deliver the finalized guest list, which he could easily have sent by email. He seemed determined not to avoid the subject, as he called out to her from the reception area in his booming politician's voice.

"Hey, Taryn, where's your better half?" He laughed and made a placating gesture with his hands when she appeared in her doorway. "Calm down, calm down. I'm talking about Sasha, not Bonnie."

"Oh, did you finally ask Bonnie on a date?" Angie asked as Taryn reluctantly dragged herself out of her office. "I told you your flirting would improve. Just like riding a bike, you know. But who's Sasha?" She turned back to Marty. "From no love life to two women in only a couple of weeks. Our Taryn doesn't do anything by halves."

"Sasha is a cat," Taryn said, wondering why she had gotten out of her bed this morning. It had been so nice there.

Warm and cozy and gloriously free of both Marty and Angie. Free of Bonnie, too, which was its most disappointing feature lately, but Taryn let that thought flit through her mind without lingering because she didn't want Marty or Angie somehow seeing it displayed in her expression. "And Bonnie and I are not dating. We're working together in a very professional way on the adoption event and on the wedding I *was* planning, but just now decided to quit."

"Wait, *you* have a cat?" Angie asked, with even more disbelief in her voice than when she thought Taryn was dating two women.

"I don't, but I could if I wanted," Taryn said indignantly. She'd be a great cat owner. Well, maybe not great, but certainly borderline mediocre. She had watched a lot of cat videos online, after all. "She just sits on me when I go to the café."

"Ah, yes, I've noticed white fur on you lately. She's been spending a lot of time at that café."

The last was directed at Marty again, and he nodded. "I know. She pretended it took three tries to get Bonnie to agree to have the wedding there, but I think we all know why she kept going back, and it had nothing to do with a rental contract."

"It was only two tries, and she really…Oh, I give up," Taryn said when her protests only made them laugh louder. "I'm going back in my office where there are no cats, and I would prefer that neither of you follow me. Angie, you're on probation for insubordination. Marty, my fees just doubled."

"You put me on probation last week, too. Is this double probation, or have I finished the first one?" Angie called after her as she walked back to her office. Taryn shut the door without answering. She would have liked to slam it, but she was far too mature for that.

She sat at her desk and opened the latest email from Bonnie, laughing out loud at the picture she had sent. It was a huge pile of the red, ribbony Valentine's Day pet toys with Pepper curled up on top, sound asleep. Bonnie's brief message said *I've told him not to get too attached since these are NOT staying in my house.*

Taryn covered her mouth with her hand to muffle her laughter. The toys were perfect for the speed dating theme of the event and would be an interesting visual addition to the simple color schemes of the rooms, but Taryn knew it must be grating on Bonnie to have a cartload of love-related items heaped in her house. She doubted any of the toys would be allowed back into the café when the adoption day was over. She sent a reply that she'd warn the Sumner Fire Department to expect calls about a disturbing heart-shaped bonfire behind the café after the event finished.

She could hear voices and laughter coming from the other room, and she figured Marty was telling Angie every detail about how she and Bonnie had misunderstood Lex's words. She had a feeling he was embellishing quite a bit—he spent enough time with the press that he knew how to sell a story. She'd have been better off just giving Angie the bare-bones version herself. Now, she'd never hear the end of it. She had to come up with a more effective threat than probation.

Taryn tapped her fingers on her desk, watching her inbox and waiting for a reply from Bonnie, but her café would be in the midst of the lunch rush now, and she was unlikely to stop what she was doing and check her email every few seconds. Taryn missed just talking to her, without all the virtual space between them. She wasn't even clear on her reason for avoiding Bonnie in the first place. Part of her was simply embarrassed by how defensive she'd gotten when the topic of love had come up. If any other person besides Bonnie had been next to her in the same situation, she'd have laughed it off without any fuss. When it came to Bonnie, her feelings were bordering on something more intense than mere friendship, and she had reacted to the mention of love with the same level of intensity.

The other reason she had stayed away from Bonnie and the café was because she was certain Bonnie's overreaction to the same situation was caused by a very different reason. Bonnie was prickly about the topic of love, especially when it was connected to her café, and she had protested only because she thought Lex was bringing up the cat-café-as-dating-site issue again, not because she shared any unresolved feelings for Taryn.

Taryn worried that if Bonnie put in the same amount of time analyzing Taryn's reaction as she had Bonnie's, then she might realize...

Taryn put her head down on her desk. All this obsessing about who guessed what or who was thinking what was exhausting. They were not in love, and they both had attempted to make that very clear. End of story.

She sat up again, tired of only communicating with Bonnie through the lonely medium of technology. She picked up her phone and happily called instead of texting.

"Hey," Bonnie said when she finally answered after several rings. She sounded out of breath.

"Hey," Taryn said, barely above a whisper because she didn't want Angie to overhear. She sighed and raised her voice to a normal pitch. Angie already thought they were dating, so what did it matter? "Is it busy there? You sound like you've been chasing cats."

"I was chasing a toddler who was chasing Mister Fuzzyboots. Really, you'd think parents would keep them under more control."

Taryn laughed, both at Bonnie's annoyed tone and the cat's name. "Mister Fuzzyboots? You've got to be kidding. I'll bet the other cats tease him relentlessly."

Bonnie huffed, but Taryn could hear a hint of shared laughter in it. "Fine. You think it's so easy, give me a new name for him right now. Gray and white cat. Go."

"Oh, um…" Taryn looked around for inspiration. "Stapler? Or does he look sort of curly, like he should be called Paper Clip?"

"Well done, but I think we'll stick with his old name. Besides, it suits him because he has very fuzzy little feet, don't you, handsome boy?"

She said the last few words with a rising inflection, reminiscent of the way Taryn had talked to Pepper. She assumed the cat in question was in Bonnie's arms right now.

Taryn thought it must be the first time in her life she had felt jealous of a cat.

"Wait a sec. Where are you right at this moment? Are you in the kitchen with that cat?"

"No," Bonnie said forcefully, but after a long enough pause to let Taryn know that yes, she was in the kitchen with a cat.

"Oh, fine, yes. He was upset and needed a break from all the people. He's not walking on the baking sheets or anything."

"As long as you're making more of those little tarts, I don't care if you have him rolling out the dough with his furry little paws." She paused, then moved to her reason for calling. "So, we've been working out a lot of the details for the adoption event through texts and stuff, but I thought it might be a good time to get together in person and…um, finalize our plans."

Well, there was a weak-ass euphemism if she'd ever heard one.

"Yes, I'd like that," Bonnie said without hesitation. Taryn smiled with relief, feeling as if something out of sync had just clicked back into place. "Did you want to come by the café? Or over to my house tonight? It's nothing fancy, but I made turkey sandwiches with cream cheese and cranberry sauce for the lunch special today, so I have a few extra to bring home."

"That sounds perfect," Taryn, surprised by how much she meant those words. They set a time to meet, and she ended the call, leaning back in her desk chair with a happy sigh.

This was turning out to be a good day. She had new clients coming for their first interview after lunch. She was ready to start planning a new wedding, since Lex and Marty's was coming along smoothly, and she always felt excited when she faced the beginning of an unknown project. And later, she'd be seeing Bonnie again. The October wedding would be here and gone before she knew it, and she didn't want to regret wasting any days between now and then by avoiding contact with her. She'd make the most of their brief relationship or friendship or whatever it was while she had the chance.

She supposed she was glad she'd gotten out of bed today, after all.

❖

Later that evening, Taryn parked along a sleepy Sumner street and walked to Bonnie's door.

She had a messenger bag full of her tablet and notes about the event slung over one shoulder. They had already managed most of the details of Finding Furever through their texts and emails, but it wouldn't hurt to go over everything once more in person, because they might have missed some nuance that would have been noticed if they were discussing this face-to-face.

Besides, the bag full of notes made this a Professional Business Meeting and not a date. Those lines were blurred where Bonnie was concerned, but Taryn didn't mind. Really, the only professional part of their relationship was the time limit set on it by their contracts. Once the wedding was over, they were both free to go their separate ways.

Of course, they could remain friends after—they lived close to each other and obviously got along well—but Taryn had already gone down that imaginary road. She didn't think she could handle seeing Bonnie with another woman, but at the same time, she wasn't prepared to have a girlfriend whose life was so tightly bound to her activist work. Especially when her cause consisted of dozens of tiny souls who needed constant care.

Taryn wasn't good at taking care of anyone but herself. She had tried with her parents and failed, and since then she'd decided she was better off focusing on her own life. She might start small with one animal or one partner someday, but she wasn't prepared to jump off the deep end into a full-time co-caregiver position to all of Bonnie's Fuzzybootses.

And so, they had tonight. And the next few months. And then Taryn would walk away.

Easy as that.

She knocked on the door, and Bonnie answered with Pepper draped over her shoulder like a serape.

"Hi. Come in," she said, pushing the screen door open and looking behind her, presumably to make sure the other cats didn't stage a getaway. "I'm glad you could make it."

"Me, too," Taryn said as she walked in and quickly closed the door behind her to prevent any escapes. "It's good to see you."

"You, too."

Yep, not awkward at all. Taryn wanted to get them back to what had become their usual easy-flowing conversations, so she tackled the big problem right away rather than avoiding it like she had been doing.

"Look, Bonnie, I'm sorry about the other day at the

tasting. That whole thing with Lex saying to be careful about falling in love to Marty and we…well, *I* overreacted. I mean, it was kind of funny the way we were so adamant about not being in love, but that only made it sound like we really are in love, which of course we're not." How many times had she used the word love? She wasn't sure, but it was time to stop. "Anyway, I know you don't want your café turned into a romantic destination, so I understand why you—"

Bonnie held up a hand to stop her, thank God.

"I'm sorry, too. You're right—I am a little oversensitive to the implication that it's somehow easy to fall in love in my café, which really is ridiculous. It's just a café, and nothing magical happens there. But still, I could have been more composed than I was."

"Yes, well, same here. Can we put it behind us?"

"Yes, please," Bonnie said with a relieved-sounding sigh.

"Good," said Taryn. "Now, let's turn to the more important topic of the evening, which is why you're wearing a kitten like a scarf."

Bonnie scratched Pepper's chin. "I'm not sure. He jumped up there while I was sitting on the couch and stayed put when I got up to answer the door. He probably sees me as a human cat tree."

"Well, it's adorable, but I'm taking him now," Taryn said, reaching to pluck the kitten off her shoulder and brushing her wrist against Bonnie's hair in the process. She wanted to put Pepper back up there just so she could do that again.

"I want to show you something," Bonnie said. She went into the other room and came back with a huge shopping bag. "I bought new beds and blankets for the Finding Furever event, since we're planning to give them to people who adopt, but I thought these fabrics might work for the wedding. I can stitch them onto the regular beds in the café, and they should last the night."

Taryn pulled out several bundles of material. Velvets and fleece, all in rich shades of purple. There were also a few lengths of silver ribbon.

"We can hem the fleece to use as blankets and cover the beds with the velvet. I hope I remembered the color correctly from your binder."

"They're beautiful," Taryn said. "And exactly the right shade. Thank you for this—I haven't had much luck finding purple cat beds online."

Taryn followed Bonnie back to the kitchen and laughed at the sight of the table. It was covered in so many bags full of cat toys and scratching posts that Taryn could no longer see any of its surface. Most of the contents were flashy red items. Bonnie put the purple fabric on a chair and poked at one of the bags.

"It's like my house has been infested with cupids. I'd rather have fleas." She shrugged. "I have to keep reminding myself it's for a good cause. We'll have to eat at the coffee table, though, unless you want to move all of this."

Bonnie got the sandwiches from the fridge and put them on plates with some chips. They ended up sitting on the floor next to the coffee table. Pepper went back to Bonnie's lap to sleep, and Taryn had Frances lying next to her. Or Alice. The first time she had come here, Bonnie had pointed out some distinguishing features between the two, but Taryn couldn't see any difference between them. Bonnie must have some sort of cat lover vision that helped her see the details other people couldn't recognize.

While they ate, Taryn walked them through her checklist for the event. She would be at the door greeting guests and handing out packets, while Jerome and Isa and other volunteers from the rescue groups would staff the rooms and serve the appetizers. Bonnie and Nancy would be floaters, moving from room to room, making sure everything ran smoothly. After everyone had visited each room, they would come back to the large conference room for dessert and a chance to watch the kitten cam, ask questions, and—hopefully—finish filling out adoption forms.

Taryn put a mark next to the last item and set the list aside. "I think we're all set," she said. "It should be an easy event since we have every detail covered."

"Says the wedding planner who usually works with humans and not felines," Bonnie said with a wry grin.

"What could possibly go wrong?"

Bonnie answered without a pause. "Oh, a cat could get loose, or a couple of them might get in a fight. One of the guests will probably be allergic and not aware of it, so they'll go into anaphylactic shock, and we'll have to call an ambulance. At least one cat will knock over a food tray or someone's glass. Someone will get scratched and threaten to sue."

Taryn grimaced. "I meant that as a rhetorical question, not a challenge."

"I haven't told you the worst one yet," Bonnie said. "This is the one that jolts me out of sleep in the night, trembling with terror. I just know Nancy is going to sneak out early, without me seeing, leaving me with the thirty cats she's bringing."

"You'd have more than fifty cats," Taryn said, trying to imagine Bonnie caring for such a massive number of them.

She wondered when it had become normal to her that Bonnie had two dozen. Fifty was ridiculous, but twenty-four? Perfectly reasonable. A few weeks ago, *one* would have seemed like too many. It was all relative, she supposed. Of course, for herself, one was still far too high a number.

"You wouldn't be able to have customers anymore," she continued. "They wouldn't fit."

"It would just be me all alone in the house, wading through wall-to-wall cats as I shuffle from food bowls to litter boxes and back again. Feeding and cleaning, feeding and cleaning. I'm definitely taking Nancy's car keys as soon as she arrives. Although that probably won't stop her from bolting. She'll think it's worth just buying another car."

Taryn's legs were going to sleep, but she didn't want to move them and disturb the sleeping cat. She settled for shifting them slightly, trying to stretch her muscles, which brought her knee in contact with Bonnie's thigh. She went still. At least with all her attention on the parts of them that were touching—albeit small and fully clothed parts—she no longer cared if all the muscles in her legs seized up. She wasn't about to move again.

"So, why a cat café?" she asked. "You were fostering and working for nonprofits. There seem to be endless ways to help cats, but this is an unusual choice."

Pepper was stretched out on his back, still sound asleep, on Bonnie's lap. She gently ruffled the fur on his belly, not making eye contact with Taryn. "I read about one in Japan and thought it sounded like an interesting concept but didn't think much beyond that at the time. Then I sort of…well…got fired from a job, and I was looking for something new, something in a different field but still helping cats, and it seemed like the right time to give it a try."

Taryn laughed in spite of herself. "Fired from a nonprofit? What could you possibly have done to deserve that? I'd assume they'd be desperate for good people, and you certainly are…I mean, you're talented and caring and competent, so who wouldn't want you?"

Taryn stumbled over those last words, but luckily Bonnie seemed even more embarrassed by the conversation than Taryn was, so she stopped caring how much her comments revealed about her feelings for Bonnie and instead watched the expressions shift across her face. She seemed to settle on trust, because she looked directly at Taryn.

"I'll show you, but you have to promise you won't laugh." Bonnie sighed, then continued. "Well, of course you'll laugh. Just not too hard, okay?"

"I promise to try not to laugh too hard," Taryn said honestly. She wasn't sure how a fire-able offense could be funny, but she didn't want to make promises she wouldn't be able to keep. Still, she'd had plenty of practice with her clients at keeping a neutral face when she felt anything but, so she'd do her best.

Bonnie reached over and grabbed her phone off the corner of the coffee table. "So, I was working for a dog rescue group in Seattle, and we had been trying to change their image to a more upscale one. They dealt mostly with purebred dogs that had been rescued or surrendered, bringing them into the city from all across the States and trying to get people to adopt them instead of supporting breeders. Anyway, I met the marketing director of one of their sponsors, a pet food company that was launching a new line of pet treats, and he asked me if I wanted to be in a commercial. I thought it might be fun to see the PR world from that angle, so I said yes."

So far so good, Taryn thought. Nothing laughable there. Quite the opposite, in fact, since with Bonnie's looks, she'd likely shine on camera. The thought of it stirred something in Taryn that was definitely not humor.

Bonnie flipped her phone over, fidgeting with it but not actually getting closer to showing Taryn anything on it. "Well, the ad was a little silly, but then someone made a GIF of part of it. Which sort of went viral." She shook her head with a groan. "Oh, Taryn, it was humiliating. The rescue group said I no longer fit with the image they were trying to project, especially since they had a fancy gala called PAWS for Wine coming up. A gala that I planned, by the way. So they fired me."

Taryn was beginning to regret how little time she spent online outside of wedding research, resulting in her lack of knowledge about which memes were viral at any given time. Bonnie seemed intent on merely talking about this GIF and not letting Taryn see it.

"I thought any advertising was good advertising, or something like that," Taryn said. "Even if they didn't realize it, then surely another group would have been happy to hire your viral self."

"Maybe," Bonnie admitted, "but I didn't try. The nonprofit rescue community is a small, niche one. Everyone would have known about me the moment I walked into an interview room, and I just couldn't handle it. I decided to start the café instead—which was the best thing I've ever done, so it worked out. But I've been trying to avoid doing anything that might bring my moment of viral infamy back to life."

"Ah. And having a publicized wedding, even if it's only a locally important one, at your café seemed too dangerous."

Bonnie nodded.

"Are you going to show me?"

She fought to keep the eagerness out of her voice when she asked the question, but she was intrigued to find out what had Bonnie so obviously discomfited.

"All right, but just remember that I didn't go into this thinking it was going to be as ridiculous as the GIF makes it seem."

She brought up the video and handed it to Taryn, busying herself with Pepper while the ad played. It was short—

mercifully—and had Bonnie dressed in what was apparently a *Cats* knock-off costume, sitting in a box with plush kittens dangling over the sides.

"And the GIF?" Taryn asked, mentally presenting herself with an Oscar for keeping her voice calm and mostly free of laughter.

Bonnie pulled it up and gave the phone back to Taryn. As she had expected after watching the ad, the short animation was the brief snippet when Bonnie said she'd do anything for a treat.

"See?" Bonnie prompted when Taryn stared at the phone for a moment without speaking. "It's ridiculous."

"Yes, well, GIF aside, at what point in this filming process did you think you were creating high art? When you did that little wiggly move?"

Bonnie gave a snort of laughter, then covered her mouth as if surprised by her own reaction. "In the dance world, we call that a shimmy," she said with unconvincing indignance.

"And are you part of the dance world?" Taryn asked, letting go of some of her control and grinning.

"Not after that ad, I'm not," Bonnie said, taking the phone and tossing it on the table with a clatter. "I know it seems funny, but I was mortified. I lost my job, and I couldn't go on a date without the person discovering this and making constant, suggestive comments about what I'd do for a treat."

Taryn finally gave in and collapsed into laughter, causing Frances—or Alice?—to walk away in a huff. "Oh, Bonnie, I'm sorry. But this is hilarious. You look so adorable in that box."

Bonnie looked torn for a moment but seemed unable to resist joining in until they were both wiping tears from their eyes. Their laughter had a slightly hysterical edge to it, as Taryn was waiting for Bonnie to get mad at her for finding the clip funny, and Bonnie seemed as if she hadn't allowed herself to see the humor in it for far too long.

Their mirth finally subsided, and Taryn reached for the phone. "I have to watch it again," she said.

"No," Bonnie said, snatching the phone from her and tossing it across the room and onto an armchair. "Trust me, it gets more appalling the more you watch it."

"This might not have fit the high-end image of that purebred group, but it's perfect for your café, you know," Taryn said as they settled back against the coffee table, shoulder-to-shoulder.

"Really? Because my café is humiliatingly ridiculous?"

Taryn heard the laughter in Bonnie's question and slapped her lightly on the thigh.

"No. Because it's a little bit silly and not mainstream or normal at all. You have to admit, having dozens of cats in a café is odd. You have more cat trees than customer chairs, and you have friends who smuggle cats in purses. But that's why people love it there, and that's why the thought of it being a place to find love is so appealing to a lot of people. You give them permission to be who they are, to be a little eccentric. And they get excited at the thought of finding somebody who will appreciate those traits, and maybe even share them."

"I guess I hadn't thought of it exactly that way before," Bonnie admitted, leaning gently into Taryn with her shoulder. "I was more focused on keeping that side of myself as far from the café as possible, but when I look at Lex and Marty, I can see what you mean."

"At least you didn't let this episode take you away from the rescue world completely. You seem born to do this."

Bonnie smiled at Taryn. "I've always loved cats because they're soft and they purr, and the people I knew in the rescue community were some of the best human beings I'd ever met. I love baking and being around other animal lovers. Plus, it's a way I can feel like I'm making a difference in the world."

Taryn felt Bonnie's words wash over her like an icy wave. She had been thinking she and Bonnie were from different worlds because of the feline equation, but maybe the gap between them was based on something far deeper and harder to bridge.

Values. Meaning.

Even in the face of what Bonnie saw as a horribly humiliating experience, she refused to give up those qualities in her life. Taryn wasn't devoting her life to rescuing helpless animals, and she certainly didn't qualify as the best human being in anyone's world. She loved what she did for a living and she was very good at it, but she wouldn't qualify as selfless in the same way Bonnie and her rescue friends did.

Bonnie reached over and slid the back of her hand gently down the curve of Taryn's cheek, and the light touch wrenched Taryn back to the present before she was able to drown in her depressing thoughts.

"Thank you for this. I've never once been able to laugh at that GIF or the ad. I still think it would make me sick to my stomach to have to watch it again, but maybe I don't feel as much dread at the thought of anyone else seeing it. You were right when you said I was sabotaging my café's success, even though my reasons were more to do with self-protection than anything else. It's been good to start letting go of that and putting the café and cats first instead."

Taryn caught Bonnie's hand before she moved it away, interlacing their fingers and resting their joined hands in her lap.

"I'm glad you're open to that, Bonnie," she said. "What you do at the café is wonderful already. Once you remove those limits you had placed on yourself, your creativity and energy are going to turn it into something even more special."

She paused for a moment, just relishing the feel of Bonnie's hand, the closeness of her, before she was going to have to pull away.

"It's good that you're open to making more money," she continued. "Especially if you're going to have fifty hungry little mouths to feed."

Bonnie laughed, but it faded away as Taryn carefully extricated her hand and stood up. "I really should be going," she said, bending to gather her notes and stuff them into her bag. "I think we have the plans sorted."

Bonnie lifted Pepper off her lap and set him on the couch before following Taryn to the door. She reached over Taryn's shoulder and held the door shut as she was starting to open it.

"What's wrong, Taryn? You changed so fast. Something changed."

Taryn turned around. Bonnie was very close, and she didn't move away. "It's nothing. I'm fine," she said, although she doubted Bonnie would let her get away with that. Bonnie just watched her silently, and Taryn sighed, looking over her shoulder and not directly at her. "It's just what you said about how amazing the rescue people are. What *good* people they are. I just don't fit in with—"

"Stop, please," Bonnie said. "Don't think you're not good enough for anyone just because you don't rescue cats or save the whales or whatever. The work you do is meaningful, too."

She rested her hands on Taryn's shoulders, her thumbs making small strokes along her neck until Taryn was barely able to focus on what she was saying.

"I remember something you said the first night you were here for dinner," Bonnie continued. Taryn hoped she wasn't about to use any long or complicated words, because her ability to comprehend anything beyond the feel of Bonnie's fingers on her skin was rapidly slipping away.

"You were talking about why you chose your job, but you said you didn't have personal experience with the kind of relationships you hope are possible, ones that were healthy and empowering and wonderful. I think you're wrong, and that you experience it every day, even if it's not romantically. Those are the gifts you give your clients when you give them the freedom to be themselves. It's a different kind of meaning you're bringing into the world than what I do, but without question, no less important. It's exactly what you just told me people want to find at my café—a place where they're honored for being who they are. You offer that, too, in a unique and beautiful way."

Then Bonnie's lips were on hers, as if she needed to physically impress what she was saying into Taryn and make her believe it. Taryn wound her arms around Bonnie's neck, holding on desperately as she started to lose herself in the sensation of having Bonnie pressed against her. The kiss was sweet and sexy and *right*…

And utterly, utterly terrifying.

Taryn planned. She organized. She didn't *feel*, and everything to do with Bonnie was about feeling. Like this kiss, which Taryn struggled to analyze and *notice* instead of letting it sweep her away.

Or the way Bonnie made her feel worthwhile and cherished and trusted on a very deep level, and the fear Taryn felt at the thought of those emotions being taken away.

It was suddenly overwhelmingly too much.

She pulled back, and Bonnie let her go. "That was…thank you for what you said. And you feel…" Taryn closed her eyes and exhaled, then looked at Bonnie again. "You feel so good.

Maybe we can…after the adoption event is done…I just need things to be slow."

She didn't want slow—her body was protesting loudly that it wanted nothing to do with slow and everything to do with fast and hard and *right now*—but kissing Bonnie, being with her, was more than just the typical physical relationship Taryn engaged in. Or, as Angie would remind her, that she used to engage in, but hadn't for a very long time. Bonnie brought out too much intensity in Taryn, but maybe, if given a little space and patience, she could find a way to handle the excess emotion. She really wanted to try.

She stepped forward and wrapped Bonnie in an embrace, trying to let her know that even though she was leaving, she wasn't running away.

She didn't want to run away, did she?

They broke apart and Bonnie smiled at her. "Slow is fine. We'll just…just wait and see where this goes."

Taryn nodded and left the house, walking down the sidewalk to her car without looking back and wondering why the warm spring air left her feeling so chilled.

CHAPTER SIXTEEN

Bonnie discovered the best way to keep her mind off her confusing romantic life—hold a fake speed dating adoption event and invite a bunch of cats.

In the days leading up to Finding Furever, she had few spare moments to think about anything beyond the event, but those moments were devoted mostly to Taryn. Just talking to Taryn about her past and showing her the humiliating social media moment had been more momentous than Bonnie had thought possible. Partly because she had felt a shift in her own perspective because of Taryn's reactions.

What had seemed huge and horrible suddenly was just goofy and a little embarrassing—maybe even, someday, entirely insignificant. Having Taryn there to share her story had made it more manageable and less awful. The thought of them sharing even more made Bonnie feel about as red and romantic as the pet toys she had bought.

Bonnie thought about their kiss, too.

She had been trying so hard to help Taryn see how worthwhile and amazing she was, and the kiss had seemed like a natural extension of the conversation. Then it had exploded into something far more arousing. For her, at least. The other thing she thought about far too often was Taryn's reaction to it.

Bonnie couldn't figure out what Taryn thought of the kiss.

She hadn't seemed repulsed, which was good, although she had also asked for them to slow down when they hadn't exactly been moving at cheetah speed up to that moment. Slowing down was basically returning to their non-kissing state, which meant keeping everything the same as it had been. Taryn hadn't seemed enthusiastic about much except for leaving the house.

In their short working relationship, Bonnie had felt more of a connection with Taryn than she ever had with anyone. It had worked both ways, too, with each of them seeming to understand the other's emotions and motivations on an intuitive level. Now, Bonnie sensed nothing from Taryn. They were friendly with each other, and they still had playful, joking moments. They weren't stiff and uncomfortable around each other, but they weren't exactly the opposite of those things either. Bonnie had no idea what was going on in their relationship or in Taryn's mind. They hadn't had another chance to talk about much beyond the event or to try a slow approach to another kiss.

Bonnie might have worried that Taryn was avoiding her if she hadn't been so busy that she really didn't have the time for either talking or kissing. She seemed to have a million details wrestling each other to get to the forefront of her mind. She was preparing food and guest packets for the event while still running her café and taking care of her cats. She fielded nearly constant calls from the rescue groups involved, asking if they could swap one cat for another or bring just one or possibly four extras, or checking if they had remembered to tell her that one of their animals inexplicably hated all calicos, so could they please not be put in the same room with one. And no, they hadn't remembered to tell her.

She had been correct when she told Taryn that the best laid plans didn't stand a chance in hell against a horde of cats.

Bonnie was relieved when the day finally arrived, and she was able to drive to the rec center with the few cats she had brought. The café was closed for the full day since she had needed to get to the venue early to oversee the decorations for the rooms and the setup of the area where guests would register and later have dessert. Then she had had to hurry back to the café and finish the prep work for the appetizers before bundling her cats into carriers and packing everything in the van she had rented.

They had planned for all the cats to start coming hours before the attendees would arrive, to give them a chance to acclimate to their temporary environment and to give Bonnie a chance to do some last-minute rearranging in the case of personality conflicts.

She made sure Mister Fuzzyboots was relaxed and comfortable in the yellow-themed room for cats that were best suited to child-free homes, then went out to the front desk where Taryn was arranging the information packets. She paused in the doorway, waiting until she had the memory of their kiss tucked as far toward the back of her mind as possible, then walked over to Taryn in the most casual, definitely-not-in-love way she could manage.

"I've had to make a couple more changes to the rooms' occupants," she said, handing Taryn her tablet with the updated list. "We have some real divas here tonight, but I think the lists are finally ready to print."

Taryn took the tablet over to the small printer she had brought from her office. "The place looks fantastic, Bonnie," she said. "You've done an amazing job here, and the guests are going to love it."

"You've done as much if not more than I have," Bonnie said. "Plus, it was your idea from the start."

They made a great team, Bonnie thought but didn't say out loud. It didn't seem like the sort of thing someone who was going slowly would say, but Bonnie knew it was true. They instinctively understood each other's strengths, and seamlessly split up and shared workloads.

"Really, all I did was…Hey. You brought Sasha and Ninja Cat?"

"Yes. They're in the red room with Jerome. He'll take good care of them."

"But you said you were only bringing a few cats," Taryn said in an accusatory tone, looking up from the list she had just printed. "You said you were only bringing some that were going to be more difficult to adopt out and would benefit from the exposure."

"Yes," Bonnie said again. She obviously knew that Salmon and Sasha were the two cats Taryn had interacted with the most at the café, but she was surprised by her response to the news that they were at the event. In the days prior, she hadn't asked Bonnie which cats she was bringing, and Bonnie hadn't had any reason to believe Taryn would really care one way or the other.

Taryn continued, "Sasha should be easy to adopt, so she didn't need to come here. She's small and friendly and cute with those spots of hers. And Ninja Cat…well, he's stealthy and protective."

Maybe Taryn just wanted to have their familiar faces greet her when she came to the café to discuss wedding plans? Bonnie wasn't sure, but she couldn't keep them from finding forever homes just so Taryn could visit them once a week.

"Exactly," she agreed, keeping her voice calm to counter the surprisingly upset tone of Taryn's. If she didn't know

Taryn ran much more complex events than this for a living, she might have guessed that she was just nervous about the evening and venting some of her anxious energy. "They're wonderful cats, and they deserve a home where they get more love and attention than I can give them in a café full of cats. The red room is for cats that are bonded pairs and need to be adopted together. It's always harder to find homes for them, so coming here will give them a better chance at being adopted."

"Did you bring Kip?" Taryn asked, sifting through the lists for the other rooms.

"No," Bonnie said. She had a feeling young Kip would find his way into a new home without needing the extra advantage of this night.

"Good, because we need him at the wedding."

"He'll be there. He's been practicing his rendition of 'Endless Love' in anticipation of the big day."

Bonnie smiled, but Taryn didn't. She always laughed at the Kip jokes, but this time she mumbled something about going to find the bathroom and walked away, leaving the pile of lists on the welcome table.

Bonnie had roughly forty-five seconds to muse over Taryn's peculiar attitude before a loud yowl had her running to the senior cat room to find that the room's volunteer had nearly tripped over one cat, but then stepped on the tail of another in her attempt to rebalance herself.

Once the affronted cat was calmed, Bonnie checked on Tulip and gave her a quick pat before leaving the room again. By the time she got back to the entrance, guests were starting to arrive. She was relieved to see a smiling Taryn at the table, handing out packets and chatting with the early arrivals.

Bonnie put the incident out of her mind. She and Taryn would hopefully find some time to sit down together and talk things out. Maybe take a picnic to Ben and Daisy's farm and eat by the river. Or get fudge at the Cannery. Anything, as long as they were together and had a chance to clear up the uncertainty that seemed to have settled between them. But tonight had to be about the cats.

She went over to her café display and made herself accessible to the people who came by to look at the photos and read about the resident cats. She had made a *Come Meet Our Cats!* brochure for the café and had put it in the info packets along with a free drink coupon.

Judging by the enthusiastic responses she was getting to her display, she had a feeling they were going to see a rise in traffic over the next few weeks. And after they showed the promo she and Jerome had filmed…well, she was both excited and a little sick to her stomach at the thought. Mainly the latter, but she wasn't going to admit it to Taryn. She was attempting to turn over a new marketing leaf, after all. And attempting to meet her past head-on and stop it from continuing to run her life.

Once the room started filling up, Jerome came in and hooked up the live feed to the café's webcams. One screen showed several cats grooming or sleeping in the late afternoon sunlight near the main dining room window. The other was the Kitten Room tea party she and Jerome had designed. The event area was already getting more crowded as they neared the start time for her nieces' big debut, and the guests clustered around the big screen like fans at a sports bar during the playoffs.

"Oh, Bonnie." Taryn had come up behind her and was now standing close by her side, her eyes on the Kitten Room screen. "It's really lovely. I feel like I'm looking through a window to the past, to a real Victorian tea party."

Bonnie smiled. That had been her exact intention with the little tableau.

Amy and Kena were wearing elaborate lace tops she had

found at the vintage clothing shop on Sumner's Main Street, with matching bows in their hair that she had made after a visit to a Puyallup craft store. She had let them choose their own leggings in bold, bright patterns, adding a modern touch to keep the scene from feeling overwhelmingly old-fashioned and inaccessible.

Jonah was in a brown double-breasted suit with a silk puff tie, looking every inch the doting father as he sat scrunched at what was clearly a children's table-and-chairs set, drinking what only Bonnie knew was apple juice out of a child-sized teacup. The scene of a father having tea with his young children was heavily staged, but their interactions were clearly genuine. They were talking and laughing in a natural way while kittens tumbled around them, playing with lacy, feathery toys.

She had always thought of Jonah as a bit of a sellout, following their parents' approved path in life. And maybe their relentless pressure and his own desire to please them had made an impact on his life choices, but watching him now, she saw something she hadn't fully appreciated before.

Yes, he had the big family her parents sanctioned, but he was far from her own father in the way he interacted with his children—not just now, when he was on display, but every time she was around him and his family. He might have chosen this life to please their parents, but she had no doubt how happy he was with it. No matter what the initial catalyst had been, he was making a life of his own.

She shifted slightly, and Taryn was right there, solid and warm and not moving away. Bonnie sighed and just rested in the moment before the chaos would begin.

When it was time to get the guests to their starting rooms, Bonnie, Nancy, and Taryn had a challenging time dragging them away from the screen and herding them to their appointed places. Once all the stragglers were out of the room, Bonnie called Jonah—watching him pull his cell out of his pocket and answer it would have definitely spoiled the vibe of the scene. He and the girls could relax until the guests returned for the dessert course. She had left them plenty of food in the kitchen to keep them occupied until they had to be back on set.

Bonnie tidied up the room, straightening photos and picking up leftover pieces of trash. Taryn still hadn't returned to the welcome desk and had probably been corralled into answering questions or escorting confused guests to the right rooms. She would have liked at least a brief moment to talk to her and to reassure herself that they were going to be all right in spite of their recent confusing up-and-down interactions, but she needed to do her assigned job. She would spend each stage of the event putting out whatever feline fires arose, so she had better get to work.

She was about to enter the first room when Jerome came trotting down the hall toward her, looking upset. She sighed. They had made it, what, two minutes before there was a problem? This was going to be a long night.

"Hey, Bonnie. Your girlfriend stole some cats."

"She's not my…wait, what do you mean she stole cats?"

"She came in the room and took Salmon and Sasha. She said you told her to get them, but when I asked why, she just left. Should I call someone? The cops?"

Well, this was unexpected. Bonnie rubbed her hand over her eyes, pulling herself together before answering.

"I don't think we need to get the police involved just yet," she said. "I'll find them. It's about time to serve the first appetizer, so you can go back to the red room. Oh, and don't talk about stolen cats in front of the guests. Or the other volunteers. Just say I needed the cats for some publicity photos or something, and I'll bring them back soon. Then get back on schedule. The show must go on, or whatever."

He still seemed concerned, but he nodded and headed back down the hall. Bonnie stood still for a moment, trying to identify what she was feeling in the midst of this unexpected crisis. Exasperated was a good word for it. She was also resisting the urge to laugh because she didn't know if she just found the situation oddly amusing, or if she was having some sort of breakdown. Most likely, it was the latter.

She turned around and headed toward the far wing of the building. They were using all the larger rooms in the rec center, but there were a few they had left empty because they were too small. She had a feeling she would find Taryn and the cats in one of them, unless she was at that moment jogging down Main Street with a big ginger cat under one arm and a small white one under the other. Bystanders might think Sumner was having another parade and line the streets to watch.

She smiled. Okay, that mental image was definitely funny. She leaned forward, resting her hands on her knees, and waited until she had her expression under control again before she started opening doors one by one in her search for the missing wedding planner-turned-cat thief.

CHAPTER SEVENTEEN

Taryn sat with her back against the wall and her legs stretched out in front of her. Sasha was on her lap, and Ninja Cat was close to her calves—close but not touching. They seemed to be handling the evening with much more composure than she was displaying at the moment, but then again, they weren't the ones who were going to have to face Bonnie's reaction once she found them.

And Taryn had no doubt she would find them soon. She wasn't really trying to hide but was merely using one of the empty rooms. The entire rec center was available for them to use, so she had every right to be here. She looked around at the bare space with only a table and a few chairs in it. She'd tell Bonnie it was the beige room, the one for cats who were perfectly fine staying at the café so didn't need to be seen and petted by the Finding Furever guests, thank you very much.

And Bonnie would eventually take the cats back to the red room. It was the inevitable result, but Taryn had just needed...

She wasn't sure what she needed. She hadn't put a lot of thought into her cat abduction, after all, but it had been a spur-of-the-moment decision. She had gone to the room just to see them and make sure they were okay—it was part of her job as event host, right?—and she had walked in to see these two traitors looking as adorable as possible, sitting side by side with their four little front paws lined up in a row, two of them tidy and small, and two a bit rough around the edges. She could practically hear the scratching of pens on adoption papers, so she had done what any completely sane person would do in that situation and grabbed the cats.

She didn't have much experience carrying one cat around, let alone two who seemed to grow increasingly aware of her lack of experience and the freedom of the empty halls that was just within their grasp as she looked for a place to hide. *Rest*, not hide, since she hadn't done anything wrong.

She somehow had managed to hold both cats while turning the doorknob to this empty room with only the thought of how Bonnie would react if Taryn's idiotic escapade led to one of her cats getting loose giving her the superhuman strength needed to accomplish the feat.

And now, she waited.

Not for long. Bonnie came into the room and carefully shut the door behind her. She sat down cross-legged on the floor.

"Hi, Taryn," she said, speaking much slower than normal. "It seems we've had a minor misunderstanding about how this event is meant to go. It's the guests who go from room to room, not the cats. The cats are meant to stay in one place."

Taryn rolled her eyes. "You don't need to talk to me like I'm a child. I obviously know I wasn't supposed to take them."

"I'm not being condescending," Bonnie continued in the same singsong tone. "I'm using a calming voice because, for the moment, I'm treating this as a potential hostage situation. Do you want to tell me what's going on?"

"Give you my list of demands, you mean?" Taryn asked with a humorless laugh. "All right, I'll play that game. I want you to take these two home. There are plenty of other cats here for people to adopt."

"So you want me to keep them at the café forever, and you can come see them whenever you feel like having a cup of coffee with Sasha in your lap and Salmon sitting next to you?"

"Yes. Is that too much to ask?" Taryn recognized the petulance in her own voice. Maybe Bonnie was right to have spoken to her like she was a child.

Bonnie sighed. "Not from me, not at all. I'd be more than happy to keep them there for you, Taryn, you know I would. But it's not fair to them, so I won't do it. They deserve more, and I really don't think you're selfish enough to keep them from it."

"But I am selfish, Bonnie," Taryn snapped, immediately getting control over her voice again when Ninja Cat's head swiveled sharply in her direction. She continued in a more sedate tone. "I live alone. I have one assistant who pretty much acts like her own boss, so it's not like you with Jerome and Isa, where you nurture them and let them use the café for school projects. I like visiting the cats, but I'm not about to bring a litter box and cat tree into my house and care for an animal every day. I take care of my clients, but only for a few months at a time, and then they go off and live their lives. I like it that way, Bonnie. I've designed my life to be simple and unsurprising. You, with your cats and your café and your selflessness, you're neither of those things."

"Ah," Bonnie said. "We're not talking about Salmon and Sasha anymore, are we?"

Taryn shook her head. She was not going to cry. "No. You know what my past was like. I spent my life trying to take care of my parents and failing. The moments of happiness when we'd act like a family and the long stretches of angry silence or shouting. I couldn't handle the swings between them, and as soon as I broke free from trying to fix them, I promised myself I wouldn't ever go through it again."

"But, Taryn, every relationship is going to have highs and lows," Bonnie said with a frown. "The healthy ones will have a lot more of those happy times, and much less intense angry ones, but you can't be together with someone without experiencing some of each."

"Exactly," Taryn said. "Which is why I don't have relationships. None that will touch me deeply enough to make me feel anything too intense, at least. I thought I could find something similar with you, something to last while we're planning the wedding, and then..."

"Something to walk away from when it's done," Bonnie finished for her. The hurt written so clearly in her expression nearly broke Taryn's resolve, but not quite. This was what Taryn needed so desperately to avoid—the pain and high emotions that came with letting anyone get too close. Right now, she was the one causing the pain, but if she stayed with Bonnie, eventually she'd be the one feeling it. She needed to break the cycle now.

"Yes," she said softly. Bonnie nodded and stared down at her hands clasped quietly in her lap. Taryn forced herself to continue. "I just can't do it, Bonnie. I'm more tempted to with you than I've ever been before, but I just can't." That was the scary part. Wanting Bonnie as much as she did only meant far too many emotions were already involved. The inevitable hard times would be even worse because of it.

"I can't even bear to say good-bye to these two, and I've barely noticed cats in the past, let alone cared about whether they wanted to sit in my damned lap or not. I'm just not like you, the way you're able to see the beauty within the pain of letting them go."

Bonnie looked up again. "I never said I wanted you to be like me, Taryn. This is a way of life I've chosen, and I'd never expect you to be involved in it if you weren't comfortable.

Besides, if we were together, you wouldn't have to worry about good-bye. I wouldn't be going anywhere."

Taryn just shook her head, her hand resting gently on Sasha's warm back, not looking away from Bonnie's face. Bonnie must have recognized her resolve, because Taryn could see exactly when Bonnie's sadness shifted to acceptance.

"All right, Taryn, I'm not going to fight you on this." She stood up and walked over to her. "You can hurt me if you need to, but I won't allow you to hurt these two by keeping them from a chance at finding a new home. We're taking them back to their room now."

Taryn nodded. Bonnie bent down and picked up Ninja Cat, leaving the room without a backward glance, expecting Taryn to do the right thing and come with her. Bonnie might not be convinced now, but Taryn was doing the right thing for herself, as well, tonight. She'd be sad for a while, but then her world would right itself again and she'd be on an even keel. Sometime soon, she hoped. She got up, clutching Sasha to her, and followed Bonnie back to the red room.

❖

If nothing else, Taryn was coming out of this evening impressed as hell with her prodigious—and hitherto unknown—acting skills.

She smiled at everyone as if her brief stint of cat thievery and her conversation with Bonnie had never happened. She helped serve dessert to their enthusiastic guests and collected far more adoption applications than they had anticipated, stowing them aside for Bonnie and not once glancing at the cat names on them.

Once everyone had returned to the main room, Jerome cut the feed to the café and played a short promo he and Bonnie had created in the past few days. Bonnie had given Taryn hints about it, but she hadn't let her see the final product until now. Taryn maneuvered through the crowded hall and into a good viewing spot—meaning one where she had a good view of Bonnie and an only slightly blocked one of the screen.

The ad started with some shots panning through the café, and then close-ups of some cats interacting with customers. After the expected feline-focused content, the camera panned past the display case full of tantalizing baked goods and over to Bonnie sitting at what Taryn would always think of as their table with an open laptop next to her. Her GIF was bouncing away on the screen before Bonnie tapped a key to pause it and looked up at the camera with a rueful, self-deprecating smile.

"We'd love to have you come by for coffee and a visit with our cats. And, of course, a locally sourced and seasonal treat or two."

When the screen switched back to the kitten tearoom, everyone turned toward Bonnie, laughing and vying for a chance to approach and talk to her. Taryn stepped back, fading into the background again. The guests' laughter sounded good-natured and friendly, and she hoped Bonnie heard it that way, too. Her smile looked a little bit forced, and Taryn knew that watching that GIF, so long a sore spot, in a public display must have been painful for her, but she seemed at ease talking to the people around her. Maybe this event would help banish that humiliating demon from her past.

Taryn busied herself handing out packets and helping attendees find their coats and bags. She should have been at Bonnie's side during the presentation—supporting her and sharing in the many successes of the night—but instead, she hovered on the edge of the celebrations, willing the night to hurry and end.

Bonnie had been adamant that no one would leave Finding

Furever with a cat in tow. The applications were filled out, and each room had regularly updated a chart with pending requests for the guests to see. But the adoptions wouldn't be processed until the days after the event, when the excitement wore down and the potential adopters would have had a chance to think about their requests and make sure they were certain about the commitment.

Taryn had accepted Bonnie's authority on that detail, recognizing her expertise in the matter, but she hadn't fully understood the emotions that would be in play until she had experienced them herself. If Bonnie hadn't intervened, Taryn might have found herself at home with her two ill-gotten felines. And as she told Bonnie, she had no intention of bringing cats into her house.

Had she, possibly, spent some time looking around her place over the past weeks and imagining where one might keep a litter box, or where the sunniest location was for a bed or two?

If she had, then it was only because she always immersed herself in whatever project she was currently planning, which just happened to involve cats this time. It was research. Nothing less. She tried to ignore the fact that she had never once looked into turtle habitats while working on the Timmy Project.

Taryn was relieved when the guests finally left—practically needing to be shoved out the doors—and she was able to take her smile down a notch from the one needed for the host of the event to one suitable for cleaning up with the volunteers. On the bright side, she didn't have to put any effort at all into keeping track of Bonnie and avoiding her. Bonnie had apparently assumed that task for herself and was doing a damned fine job of it.

What she did avoid were the cats and everyone's elated discussions about which ones had the longest interest lists, like they were gossiping over which debutantes had been asked to dance at a ball. Whenever she heard the topic come up in conversation, she immediately moved to a different area to clean, which meant she ended up ping-ponging around the room because the event had been such a success.

Taryn sighed as she edged her way out of a group when she heard the name *Tulip* come up and walked over to the dessert table to help pile up plates. On her way there, she passed the screen that was still showing the kitten room webcam.

Jonah was still sitting on his tiny chair, his tie discarded, reading a book as he presumably waited for Bonnie to return to the café. The two girls were asleep on blankets on the floor, surrounded by tiny puddles of kittens. The unscripted scene was even more adorable than the tea party, if it was possible, and Taryn thought it was a good thing the guests were no longer here to see it. As it was, Bonnie was going to need to build ten kitten tearooms to accommodate all the reservations she was going to get after tonight.

Taryn finally packed the last box in a waiting car and waved as its driver pulled away, leaving her alone in front of the rec center. She did one last sweep through the place, cringing a bit as she peered into what had been the red room—the scene of her brief but thrilling crime spree—and then she locked the glass doors. When she had first come up with the Finding Furever concept, it had been part of the ploy to get Bonnie to agree to the wedding. She had realized it was a clever idea, but in a detached way. The event had become something much more than she had anticipated, and she finally understood the impact it had on the lives of these animals and rescue workers. She was proud to have been part of it, but relieved for it to be over. Life could go back to normal now, with only the impending dread of having to face Bonnie again in October hanging over her. She'd go back to the all-virtual mode of communication with her until then.

She went home and let herself into her house. There was no litter box to clean, no food bowl to fill, no cat to trip her up.

No Bonnie to talk to or kiss or follow into the bedroom.

Yes, life was back to normal. What a relief.

CHAPTER EIGHTEEN

Bonnie let herself into the café earlier than normal on Friday morning, almost a week after Finding Furever had taken place.

Already, the space felt emptier to her, even though she had brought so few cats to the event that their number hadn't reduced significantly yet. She had spent the week conducting interviews with the applicants, and three of her cats had been tucked into traveling crates and sent to their new homes.

So far, she *had* noticed a real change in the interviews compared to her previous ones. The people she talked to had a greater sense of why they had chosen each particular cat, and how the animal would match their lifestyles. The educational side of the event had had clear results, and she was already brainstorming ways to incorporate the ideas into daily life at the café, both through displays on the walls and an interactive *What Cat Is the Right Fit for Me?* quiz on the website.

She still didn't believe her café was necessarily a good place to make love matches between humans—she was living proof of its failure in that regard—but making the best matches possible between adopter and cat was worth striving for. She had two more adoption interviews set for the weekend, and hopefully far more in the future.

And while her cat population had diminished slightly, her customer base had noticeably grown. She recognized some faces from the event, and most of them had brought friends or family who hadn't been there. She also heard from several new customers that they had been told about her café by friends who had been at the adoption event, and they just had to come see her place for themselves.

She was tempted to enjoy the windfall while it lasted and let it die out naturally, but she had started trying to push herself past those initial, habitual responses. She had put them in place to protect herself, but why bother now? She had been hurt by Taryn in a way that made the pain she had felt when the whole social media humiliation episode had first happened seem like a stubbed toe compared to a compound fracture.

Now, she needed to remain proactive, not just be glad the event had gone well and stop there, but throw her energy into planning another. Taryn's advice to act the part of her former marketing persona and treat herself as a client was more effective than she had expected. She was more objective than before, and more determined to seek out opportunities to promote her café rather than passively and reluctantly accept them if they happened to her.

She had faced some jokes about the GIF, but they were oddly anticlimactic now and barely bothered her. Taryn had both helped to ease Bonnie's reaction to the past and numb her to the present. She had treated the clip as something silly and cute—on par with the café's playful cats and themed coffee names—which had led Bonnie to rethink her panicked attempts to keep it hidden forever. And her breakup had made Bonnie lose all concern about what other people might think or say about it. What had once been a huge embarrassment, worthy of getting fired over, now seemed like a funny lark and newfound publicity opportunity. She was proud about how she could look at the GIF objectively now.

She lost her sense of objectivity when it came to thoughts of Taryn, however.

After their awful talk in the spare room, she had felt her initial sadness get washed out by a numb feeling that had carried her through the rest of the night. She'd had so much to do at the event and directly after. And once they got back to the café, she and Jerome and Isa, Jonah and the sleepy girls, had gathered in the main room and rehashed every moment of the event—at least the publicly known ones—while the cats settled around them. Luckily, Jerome had kept his promise about not discussing the cat theft with anyone, so Taryn didn't come into the conversation much at all.

It was when she had gotten home that the numbness had worn off completely, and her sadness returned with a vengeance.

She had been crying on and off since, and she had taken the adoption good-byes harder than ever. After each one, she had found herself at home, sobbing on her bed with Pepper in her arms, Frances and Alice pressed against her. As much as she hated to admit it, she was beginning to understand Taryn's point about not wanting to experience strong emotions. They hurt. They were hard to take. But they were far better than the alternative—the lonely effort required to maintain emotional equilibrium.

Bonnie just couldn't live without risking sadness in order to give joy a chance. Even the hurt she was experiencing now came with the memories of how much she had enjoyed Taryn's company when they had spent time together. The jokes and laughter, the process of uncovering and learning about Taryn's past and what made her the woman she was today. Bonnie couldn't bring herself to pretend she would give those up if it meant removing the pain she felt now. She was passionate about the work she did for her cats, accepting the wrenching pain of letting them go when they had their chance, because of the happiness they brought to her life while they were with her and the opportunity she had to repay them by finding them loving homes.

She was passionate about Taryn, too. More than she had fully realized, and now she would never get to know how deep that passion could have become.

She fed the cats on autopilot and went through her usual morning routine at the café. A contractor was coming by soon to talk about expanding into the backyard, so she was trying to get all her chores finished by then.

She was coping well. Yes, she was sad, but she didn't think anyone else had noticed. If anything, they probably thought she was doing better than ever as she pushed forward with numerous plans for the café, like the new rooms for the Kitten Teas. Then she and her three could move in and, well, life would go on.

Bonnie had premade the batters and doughs for most of the morning baked goods last night—for once skimping only slightly on freshness to give herself time to meet the contractor—so she only had to fill trays and muffin tins and pop everything into the ovens. By the time Isa arrived, she had the front cabinets filled and ready for customers.

"Good morning," she said in what she hoped was a cheery voice, but ended up sounding a little weird to her ears. She toned it down a bit. "I'll be out back with Andrea this morning, but if it gets too busy, just come get me, okay?"

"Yes, I remember," Isa said, speaking more slowly than usual. "You told me six times yesterday and texted me about it this morning."

Had she? She thought she remembered mentioning it once yesterday. Isa was probably exaggerating. "Well, good, then. You know where to find me if you need me."

"Yes, Bonnie. In the backyard."

Bonnie frowned, wondering if Isa was having a bad day. She'd have to remember to ask her about it later, but right now she had other business that needed her attention. Andrea's truck had just pulled into a parking place out front, so Bonnie needed to focus on this project first.

Andrea came through the café and was given coffee and a croissant by Isa, and then she and Bonnie went out into the yard. Bonnie tried hard to focus on everything Andrea said, but her mind felt a little foggy. The effort of keeping Taryn out of her thoughts seemed to be causing some of her brain cells to explode in little puffs, hiding everything else from view.

This was her pet project, though—it had been her dream ever since the first Kitten Teas had been so well received.

She managed to drag her awareness into the yard and out of her imagination, where she and Taryn were having that picnic by the river she had planned to suggest. Where they could have talked out their issues in a calmer place, without the stress of the adoption event intensifying everything to an overwhelming level. And then they could have—

She startled, suddenly aware that Andrea had asked her a question. What had it been? Something about windows?

"Oh yes," Bonnie said, the words finally penetrating her mind. She walked over to the side fence. "I'd like the larger windows to be low and face this direction. I thought we could put a few chairs and tables out here, so customers can walk by and observe the kittens when we aren't having teas in there, or sit down here and watch them. We'll need the windows to be low enough for a seated person to see in. And maybe ledges or window seats on the inside."

Andrea made more notes and then left with a promise to come back the following week with an estimate and information about the permits they'd need. Bonnie walked her out through the gate and then entered her café again from the front.

There were a few people at the tables already, and Bonnie was surprised to see Viv and Jerome sitting in the back. At Taryn's table. The image of her sitting there with Sasha in her lap hit Bonnie hard. She was going to need to move that table. Maybe replace it with some new cat trees to hide the entire area from view. Or ask Andrea to just tear down the whole wall.

She walked over and her friend stood up to give her a hug. "Hi, Viv. What are you doing here? And Jerome? You don't start work for hours."

"Have a seat, honey," Viv said. "I just came by to see how you're doing. So did Jerome."

Strange. Bonnie sat on the edge of the chair Viv had pushed her toward. Isa joined them, handing Bonnie a ceramic mug.

"Your usual," she said, sitting next to Jerome. He kicked her leg in a not-so-subtle way. "Oh, right," she added. "Remember that although the image of a cat drinking a bowl of cream is a charming one, dairy products aren't good for them."

She said the phrase in a cheerful voice. Given that she usually delivered the mini-lesson somewhat sulkily, Bonnie didn't fully believe the cheer. She sniffed at her drink.

"Is this made with cream?"

"No, almond milk like normal. Okay, then, remember that dairy alternatives aren't good for cats."

That was more like her normal delivery. "You're all acting kind of odd," she said. "I'm not sure what's—"

"Sorry I'm late," Nancy said breathlessly, coming up

behind her. "Hey, Bonnie, aren't you going to ask me what's under my coat? Maybe try to kick me out of the café?"

Nancy was wearing a long trench coat and holding it closed with her arms around her middle. There was an obvious lump of squirming cat under there.

"Another cat, I'm assuming?" She held out her hands. "Fine. Give it here. A few have gone to new homes, so I have some space."

Nancy looked at the others. "Oh, dear, she really is bad, isn't she? Hang on for about a half hour. I'm going to run home and bring a few more here before we fix her."

A chorus of protests stopped her, and she sat down with a huff after extricating the cat and handing it to Bonnie. She was big and healthy looking, with a shiny black coat. Of course. A cat to remind her of Taryn and her Halloween wedding plans. Bonnie hugged the cat to her, admitting to herself that almost any cat would remind her of Taryn now. Gingers and white cats and ones with stripes. Black cats and tuxedoes and torties. Gray striped kittens like Pepper or, really, any kitten at all.

"We're worried about you, Bonnie," Viv said. "Apparently you've been a little forgetful and absent-minded."

"I have not," Bonnie said.

"You have. You just keep forgetting about it," Jerome said unhelpfully.

"Look in the bakery case," Isa added. Bonnie looked over and saw a carton of orange juice next to the trays of Danishes. She had used it to make a glaze for her cranberry muffins that morning and had thought she had returned it to the fridge. And was that her coat?

"Those are decorative elements. I'm just trying to give the place a little more style."

"Your socks don't match," Viv said.

Bonnie sighed, tired of this game. Tired in general. "It's all the rage in Paris. Look, I appreciate the obnoxious meddling, but I'm fine. Just a little tired."

"And a lot heartbroken," Isa said.

"I told them about the cat thief," Jerome admitted. "The two of you seemed to like hanging around together, but we haven't seen you together since that happened. She brought the cats back, so maybe you can forgive her."

Okay, so he had broken his promise and blabbed to the very people who had no boundaries when it came to butting in to her personal business. She'd fire him if she could only find the energy.

"I'm not mad at Taryn about taking the cats. She was just sad about them being adopted and wanted to spend some time with them before it happened. And now that the event is done, we don't really have any need to keep seeing each other. I'm fine."

Her last statement echoed the lie Taryn had told her before she admitted what she was really feeling that night at Bonnie's. Before the kiss. The words weren't true for Bonnie right now, either. She looked around the table at her friends.

"No, I'm not fine. And yes, Isa, maybe I am a little heartbroken. But I promise I will be fine eventually, so just bear with me for a while longer."

"Of course you'll be fine again," Nancy said briskly. "You'll mope for a couple more days, and then you'll snap out of it, because people in our line of work are tenacious as hellhounds and twice as strong." She paused and patted Bonnie on the arm. "Which means I have a couple more days to get as many cats in here as possible. I'll have to work fast..."

Bonnie looked at Jerome. "Now is the time to call the cops."

They all laughed, looking relieved to hear her make a joke. She loved these people. They had been able to make her recognize how poorly she had been coping, even though she thought she was hiding it from everyone but her own cats, when she cried at night. She didn't feel embarrassed by this chat they had arranged. They only wanted her to understand how her sadness was affecting her life, and to know that they were here for her until she pulled herself together again.

Viv reached over and scratched the black cat under her chin until Bonnie felt the rhythmic vibrations of her purrs. "She's very pretty," she said. "What's her name?"

Bonnie scanned the room, her eyes coming to rest on the condiment area by the register. "Sugar," she said as the cat's audible purrs grew louder. She exchanged a glance with Nancy, who tilted her chin in a *go on* sort of gesture. Bonnie turned back to Viv.

"And she really seems to like you. It's as if the two of you share a special bond…"

Chapter Nineteen

Taryn squinted, as if it would help her see more clearly through the mesh mask, and aimed the stream of smoke from her can in the direction Ben was pointing. It would have been much easier without the heavy gloves she was wearing, but she had been stung by a single bee a few times in the past, and each one had hurt like hell. She could probably fit a hundred of these wee honeybees on one hand, and she did not want to find out what that many stings felt like.

"That's it, little ones," she muttered as the smoke filtered down through the frames. "Just go to sleep. Don't worry about the enormous human hovering over your box."

She heard Ben's chuckle, and then he took the smoker from her. "Now grasp the frame here, in these grooves, and gently pull it out. Be careful not to tilt it, but lift straight up. Good. Just hold it there for a moment."

He delicately brushed the groggy bees that remained on the waxy surface back into the box, then used one gloved finger to swipe along the frame. Deeply golden honey oozed out where he had removed the whitish covering.

"Wow, it's real honey," she exclaimed, then smiled at how silly she sounded. She knew what bees were and where honey came from. It was somehow different standing here, where she was playing a small part in the process rather than picking up a jar in the grocery store.

He nodded, seeming to understand what she was saying. "We're held at a distance from most of our food in the modern world. I never fully appreciated what was on my plate until I experienced firsthand how much effort and how many steps it takes to get from a seed to a piece of produce, or from a flower to a pot of honey." He led her several yards away. "You can take your mask and gloves off now, and taste this."

She pulled off the canvas hood and gloves, sighing as a slight breeze cooled her skin. She was sweating in the sunshine, and when she licked some of the honey off her finger, she could taste sun and heat and a fruity sweetness.

He went back and replaced the lid, then they returned to the production shed where Daisy was waiting for them. She put small pieces of oozing honeycomb on top of wedges of bread and carried it over to a small metal table.

Taryn took a bite and melted a little inside. Nutty brown bread and honey was about as simple a dish as one could make, but the flavors were complex and delicious. Last night she had eaten a take-out cheeseburger, which had tasted exactly like the one she'd had the night before.

She was in a rut, but she wanted it that way, didn't she? Predictable flavors, predictable routines. This offering from Daisy and Ben made her taste buds clamor for more, though, and she liked the new sensations.

She could hear Bonnie in her mind, wryly telling her to be careful about getting too excited over the food, because she was going to feel proportionately sad when the plate was empty.

She tried to tell imaginary Bonnie that experiencing an intensity of flavors in what she ate was completely different from experiencing intensity and passion in love. One was a pleasant diversion, while the other was really scary.

Bonnie told her she was full of shit.

Or maybe she said that to herself. She wasn't sure. She carried on far more conversations in her head than made her comfortable, but it was the only way she had to ease the pain she felt in Bonnie's absence. Knowing she was solely responsible for them being apart did not help, especially since the Bonnie in her mind took any opportunity to remind her of it.

Yes, she was definitely losing it, she decided as she took another piece of bread.

She saw movement out of the corner of her eye and turned, spotting a fluffy gray cat with a white face and paws on the far side of the shed. "Oh, you have a cat," she said, feeling a rush of sadness. No, she reprimanded herself sternly. Nostalgia. That was all it was. She hadn't been around any cats since the adoption event...

And whose fault is that? Annoying Imaginary Bonnie asked.

Ben looked over at the cat. "Yes, we have about five of them. Bo—" Daisy made a kind of cross between a squeak and a grunt, and he abruptly truncated her name. "Sorry, I mean a friend of ours brought them here."

"Yes, that was much better," Daisy said with a laugh. "Sorry, Taryn. I suppose we shouldn't coddle you. Bonnie told us some of what happened between you—no details, but enough to let us know that things didn't work out for the two of you. Anyway, before I interrupted Ben, he was saying that she and some other volunteers often trap feral cats, get them neutered and spayed, then rehome them as barn cats if they can't be safely returned to their colonies. Two of ours have gotten reasonably friendly with us, and the others just want to be left alone. We feed them and give them a safe, warm place to live, and they keep our barns free of mice and rats."

Naturally, Bonnie found time in her hectic week to search out more cats to save. Taryn felt an undeniable rush of pride for her. "She's amazing," she said softly. "Is she…is she doing okay?"

"Tell us more about this wedding you're planning," Daisy said gently.

Taryn nodded, accepting the boundary Daisy had just placed around her friendship with Bonnie even though she wanted to press for more information. Was Daisy refusing to answer because Bonnie was miserable without her, or because she had moved on and was deliriously happy with someone else? Or was she simply telling Taryn to mind her own business because she had given up the right to ask about Bonnie? None of them were appealing options. She wanted Bonnie to be happy in a neutral, not-dating-anyone-else sort of way.

She startled a little as she realized that was what she had wanted for Sasha and Ninja Cat, too. For them to be reasonably okay and not attached to anyone but her—and not too attached to her because she had her own life to live. Well, that wasn't a flattering bout of self-reflection.

Ben and Daisy were watching her patiently, apparently giving her time to get herself together and talk about her reason for coming here. Or her somewhat contrived reason for coming here, when the truth was she had wanted to be close to anything and anyone that reminded her of Bonnie but wasn't actually Bonnie herself.

Yikes. These internal monologues were getting overly harsh. And far too accurate for comfort.

"They're a couple in their fifties," she said, finally moving on to the topic at hand. She watched the gray cat make his slow way around the perimeter of the building as she spoke. "They came to me because they have both been married before and didn't want to go the same traditional route, but they don't have a clear picture of what they *do* want. When I interviewed them, though, they kept using phrases like fresh start and how their love grew after they had been friends for a long time. When clients need me to help them focus their theming, I'll often ask about favorite colors, and they both mentioned spring green. I just had a mental picture of them standing in a field between rows of new growth, saying their vows while the world is coming back to life around them. I know it sounds corny, but I think they'd love to get married in a place like this, when there are baby animals everywhere and everything is turning green."

She looked at Ben and Daisy, who were now holding hands as they listened to her. Ben wiped a hand briefly across his eyes.

"That doesn't sound corny at all," he said. "It sounds absolutely beautiful. I can think of several fields that would work, depending on the exact date, of course."

"And we'll have the barn available, in case it rains," Daisy added. "They can have chicks and goat kids in their wedding photos, too. You know, renting the place out for weddings might be something we should look into doing regularly, especially if they're scheduled for slower seasons on the farm."

Taryn smiled as she watched them start bouncing ideas off each other. Every word she had said about the interview with the couple had been true, but she could have taken this proposal to any number of local farms. She had come here to feel closer to Bonnie in an oblique way. In fact, she knew of a few farms that already did regular weddings and anniversary or birthday parties, but she had only been able to picture her clients at this one. She gave Ben and Daisy the names of the others, though, so they could check out their websites and get more ideas.

How very different this was from her first discussions with Bonnie, when she fought like a killer bee against using her café for anything that risked publicity and exposure of her past. Most people wouldn't think that being open to advertising a business was a sign of bravery, but Taryn knew better. She understood how much Bonnie had needed to overcome to get to a place where she was willing to accept her past mistakes and allow both financial success and love into her life. Taryn wasn't sure she had strength enough to take the same leap and let passion into her own.

Imaginary Bonnie called her a coward and disappeared.

❖

Later, Taryn sat at her desk and typed out some of the ideas she, Daisy, and Ben had thought of during their visit.

She had a good sense for couples after doing this for so many years, and she had no doubt her new clients were going to love every ounce of this proposal. She was excited by the prospect, too. It was another of those ceremonies that would benefit from its setting, organically enriching the vows that were spoken, just like the homey café and the cats would add emphasis to the love and family Lex and Marty were creating together.

She felt a twist in her stomach at the thought of their wedding since she wasn't sure she'd be able to go to the café without breaking down. She might have to send Angie in her place.

She heard a tap on her door and looked up as Angie herself came in and handed her a large paper to-go cup. Taryn thanked her before taking a sniff. Chamomile tea. Or maybe

Catmomile. Chameowmile? Yes, that was better. She smiled and took a sip as Angie settled into the chair opposite her.

"Are you ready to talk about it yet?" Angie asked.

"I don't know what you mean, but I doubt it."

"I mean, talk about what happened between you and your Bonnie."

Taryn sighed. All the Chameowmile in the world couldn't make her relaxed now. "She's not *my* Bonnie, and I thought I told you I'd put you on probation if you mentioned her name again."

Angie waved her hand dismissively. "Sorry, but I've got four probations going at the moment, so I really can't juggle another one."

"There's nothing to talk about. We weren't even dating, not really. A couple of business dinners, one kiss." Taryn shrugged, as if the one kiss hadn't sent her into such a tailspin she'd had to run away. Yes, like a coward. "We decided mutually that we are better off keeping our relationship as a professional one. It was the mature decision to make."

"By mutually, do you mean that you decided this?"

"Maybe," Taryn admitted.

"And how exactly is your life better without her in it? Because from where I sit"—Angie gestured toward the reception area—"I think you're looking awfully mopey for someone who's experienced a suddenly improved quality of life."

"Better in the long run is what I meant," Taryn said weakly. Yes, her life felt worse now, but she'd eventually get over the pain and go back to whatever she had been before Bonnie, wouldn't she? She'd get back to being steady and unruffled by life. A little lonely, maybe, which would only be harder to take now because the memory of Bonnie wasn't going away.

Lonely without knowing exactly what she was lonely

for had been easy to bear, but now she knew. She had tried to protect herself from being hurt in a relationship, but all she had done was take away everything hopeful and fun and wonderful she'd had with Bonnie and replace it with sadness without her. At least her misery was steady and predictable, just like she'd wanted.

Angie watched her in silence, then softly asked, "And what about this Sasha?"

Taryn sighed. "I told you, she's a cat. Not a woman."

"I remember. But seems like she might be a relationship you can handle, since you don't seem prepared to cope with a human one."

"I could cope if I wanted to," Taryn protested, but her mind had wandered somewhere else, to a place where it went every night when she went home.

She pictured going back to her house after work and walking inside to be greeted by Sasha's husky purrs and freely given love, love that Taryn didn't need to plead for or earn by being perfect. It was just there, ready to be shared. Bonnie had offered the same thing, without expecting Taryn to be anything but herself, and she had rejected it. She knew what rejection felt like, and she hated that she had inflicted that on Bonnie.

Yes, Sasha would fill some of the void Taryn had intentionally tried to create, but she wasn't enough. Taryn wanted Ninja Cat, too. And most of all, she wanted Bonnie.

"Oh, honey, you're making this far too difficult when it should be the simplest thing in the world." Angie came around the desk and handed Taryn a tissue. She stared at it blankly for a moment before realizing she was crying. "You want a cat, go sign the adoption papers. You want Bonnie back, go tell her so. In all my time here, I've never seen you be anything but confident and determined. You don't let fear rule you at work, so why are you letting it take charge of your love life?"

Angie returned to her chair and sat down with a thump.

"Honestly. You finally found a woman who seems willing to put up with you, so for God's sake, don't let her get away."

"Hey," Taryn said. "I'm charming. Any woman would be glad to have me."

Angie nearly doubled over in laughter at Taryn's comment. She sighed and wiped her eyes with the damp tissue. Imaginary Bonnie and Angie would probably get along very well. Taryn was getting a bit sick of both of them.

CHAPTER TWENTY

Bonnie rolled out her dough and trimmed it into neat discs, placing each one into a pie pan and crimping the edges. She repeated the process until all the pans were done, then sprinkled chopped broccoli and ham into the bottoms of them. Finally, she poured a whipped mixture of eggs, cream, and herbs nearly to the rim and covered the whole mess with shredded Gruyère.

Not one single step should have brought Taryn to mind, but Bonnie hadn't stopped thinking about her during the entire process. Okay, admittedly she hadn't really stopped thinking about her since the first time they met, but it had been worse this morning. All because they had eaten quiche together one time for dinner at Bonnie's. Now, she had to either stop making them completely, which would upset her customers since this was a favorite lunch special, or just accept that she was going to have Taryn in her thoughts more intensely than usual for a couple of hours every week.

Bonnie gently slid the quiches into the ovens one at a time, careful not to spill any of the egg mixture. She set her timer and looked around for her next task. Cookies, yes. She gathered the ingredients, picking white chocolate and macadamia nuts as the flavor of the day, and got to work.

While still obsessing over Taryn.

She had come out of her funk after about two weeks, returning to some semblance of being a functioning human being. She no longer repeated instructions to Jerome and Isa numerous times, and she hadn't put any of her clothing in the bakery case for days now.

Progress.

Internally, she felt about the same—no less lonely or hurt—but she assumed she was seeming more normal to everyone around her. If she wasn't, she was sure they would have sat her down for another intrusive chat session, and Nancy would have tried to smuggle in another cat.

It was for the best that Bonnie learned how to act perfectly fine because she had a feeling she wasn't going to be anything approaching that for a long time.

She made a huge batch of cookie dough in her industrial-sized mixer, then folded in the nuts and white chocolate by hand. She scooped the dough onto baking sheets, observed the entire time by Kip, from his usual perch on the far counter. She either needed to bring a bed in here for him or get firmer about enforcing the no cats in the kitchen rule. He was just such good company, she hated the thought of shooing him out to the main room every time she baked.

She ran through the checklist she had written on the whiteboard before pulling ingredients for a salad made with spring greens fresh from Ben and Daisy's farm out of the fridge. She tossed it with some dressing and portioned it out into small bowls, before making a few dozen individual fruit and yogurt parfaits. She had just put the last of them on a tray to bring out to the counter when Isa came through the door.

"I'll take those," she said, sounding unusually subdued. "There's someone who wants to fill out an adoption form out there. I thought maybe you should handle this one."

"Sure," Bonnie said, washing her hands and drying them on some paper towels. "Listen for the timer, though, will you? The quiches only have another fifteen minutes or so to cook."

She held the door open for Isa to come through with the parfaits, then turned toward the register. Luckily Isa had already made it through the door because Bonnie might have unintentionally slammed it on her when she saw Taryn standing near her old table. Bonnie knew she should have had that whole damned area demolished.

She might have stood frozen in place for the rest of the day if Isa hadn't given her a hard shove, knocking her off balance and making her take a step forward. She took a deep breath and continued walking.

"Hi, Bonnie," Taryn said quietly when she reached her. She had seemed so polished and elegant the first time Bonnie had seen her. Now she was no less beautiful, no less tidily put together, but she looked raw, somehow. Bonnie wondered briefly if Taryn was aching as much as she was. She shook herself mentally. No, she wasn't. Otherwise she would have come back before now.

"What do you want, Taryn?" she asked. They had exchanged several terse emails about the wedding plans, and Bonnie saw no reason why they shouldn't continue to use that convenient, distant form of communication.

Taryn paused as if struggling to find the right words to use. "I want to adopt a cat," she said, her sentences rushing out of her now. "Two cats. Sasha and Ninja Cat. Salmon. I've been studying how to take care of them, by reading books and things, not just by watching cute cat videos on YouTube. I have a vet, and here's the receipt for all the stuff I bought them."

She faltered to a stop, and even though Bonnie wanted to yell at her or tell her to get out and adopt a cat from Nancy if she really wanted one, the earnest expression on her face broke through Bonnie's hurt and anger. Taryn looked as desperate as she had in that small room at Finding Furever, but there was something else there, too. Hope. Determination.

"Oh, Taryn," she started, not quite sure what to say now that they were so close together. She had imagined having a conversation with her, but this wasn't the one she had planned.

Taryn watched Bonnie with her brows pulled together, then her expression shifted and she looked about to cry. "Oh, they're already gone, aren't they. I waited too long, and now—"

"No. No, they're still here," Bonnie reassured her. She reached out and put her hand on Taryn's arm, guiding her toward a chair. "Sit down, okay? Talk to me about what's going on."

They sat at the table, and Taryn set down the receipt she had brought from the pet store. Bonnie picked it up and scanned through the items.

"Exactly how many cats are you trying to adopt?" she asked. "You seem to have bought enough things for at least a dozen."

"I think just the two to start," Taryn said with a sniff. "Maybe I'll work my way up from there."

She gave a small laugh, and Bonnie felt an answering smile on her own face. "You're really serious about this?"

Taryn nodded. "More than anything."

Bonnie shrugged. "Wait here, then, and I'll get the adoption form. I have to warn you, though, the interview isn't easy to pass."

She went into the kitchen and leaned against the counter, giving herself a moment to regain her composure. This seemed unreal. Maybe she was back to her foggy state and just hallucinating the whole encounter. Maybe she was dreaming and would wake up and—

"Why are you hiding in here?" Isa hissed at her, coming

into the kitchen. "Get back out there and give her a piece of your mind. Let her know she had no right to hurt you the way she did, and she's not welcome in here anymore. Or kiss her and win her back." She paused and tapped her fingers on the counter. "Either way, you probably should let her adopt the cats first. She seems nice, and I believe she really wants them."

"That was all very helpful. Thank you," Bonnie said sarcastically, pushing herself upright. She grabbed a clipboard and an adoption form and went back into the dining room. She still wasn't sure which of those options she was going to choose. They all had their merits, although kicking her out seemed the least risky. Kissing her, while tempting, held too much chance she'd get hurt again.

First, she'd hear what Taryn had to say. Then she'd decide.

❖

While Taryn waited impatiently for Bonnie to come back, she scanned the room, searching for her cats.

Her cats.

She had been living with the idea of adopting them for a while now, but it had taken her days to work up the courage to come back here. Even though she had made the decision to try not only for Sasha and Ninja Cat, but for Bonnie, too, her old fears hadn't been easy to shake. She had driven by the café several times, only to leave Sumner again and go back to her office, where she had to face Angie's dramatically disappointed sighs.

But now, here she was. Intentionally heading toward the type of intense emotional moment that she always tried to avoid, because no matter the outcome, she was about to face either the highest or the lowest moment of her life.

Bonnie came back to the table holding a clipboard and

pen. Taryn reached for them to fill out the papers, but Bonnie shook her head. "I'll take care of it. Just answer the questions."

"Can I see the cats first?"

Bonnie frowned. "I don't think that's a good idea," she said slowly. "Especially considering your prior offenses."

"My prior...Hey, I was just giving them a sightseeing tour of the rec center."

Bonnie smiled, and Taryn wondered if she'd get extra points on the adoption form for that. She gestured toward the window. "They're over there. Isa, if she tries to leave the café, throw a scone at her head."

"Sure thing, boss," Isa called from over by the counter.

Taryn shook her head and walked in the direction Bonnie had indicated. A fleece-lined basket was hanging from the windowsill, and when she looked inside it she saw a patchwork pile of ginger, white, and stripey fur. She couldn't see any heads, which was alarming, but as she got closer, Sasha's popped out from under Ninja Cat's ginger arm, and she gave Taryn a mix of a yawn and a meow before she closed her eyes again.

Taryn smiled and walked back to the table, with no attempts at cat theft. If Bonnie denied her application, though, she might return to her life of crime.

She sat down. "Okay, I'm ready."

Bonnie looked at her clipboard, tapping her pen on its edge. "All right, first question. Are you single?"

"It doesn't really ask that, does it?" Taryn tried to turn the clipboard so she could see the page, but Bonnie held it close.

"It actually does. We always ask how many people are in the household. Kids, other animals. How many people will be acting as caretakers for the cats."

"I'm not sure. Can you write *in process*?"

Bonnie looked at her quizzically. "What's in process?"

"The household. Can you put a range, say from one to twenty-some? I'm still ironing out the details."

Bonnie shook her head silently and looked at the form again. "Okay, next question. Any felonies? I'm just going to check yes for that one."

Taryn snatched the clipboard before Bonnie could stop her. She set it on the table and rested her elbows on it, leaning forward. "Bonnie, I want these cats in my life. I want you in my life, too, and your three cats, and all the ones here, and I suppose Isa and Jerome, too. The whole package. I don't care how many interviews it takes, or how many forms you invent, I'm not going to stop trying."

Bonnie stared at her, her face expressionless. "Animals can be heartbreaking, Taryn. I don't think you quite grasp how much you'll come to care for them, and how frightening it might be if something goes wrong and they get hurt or sick. I don't want to send them home with you if you're going to abandon them when emotions get too high, or when it's not all snuggles and purrs."

"Ah," Taryn said, echoing Bonnie's words from the night of Finding Furever. "We're not talking about the cats anymore, are we?"

"Not just the cats, no."

"Bonnie, I pushed you away because I was afraid of feeling too much for you, but I was too late. I already loved you. Walking away, being away from you—that hurt more than anything, but you know what? I survived it. I hated it, and I'll do whatever I can to keep from feeling that loneliness again, but I learned that I'm strong enough to handle whatever comes."

Bonnie was silent for a moment, still not revealing her

reaction to Taryn's words, but her eyes looked misty. She looked around the café. Several tables were occupied. "Can we finish this interview in private?" she asked.

Taryn nodded, following Bonnie through the door and into the kitchen, trying to ignore Isa's knowing smirk as they walked past.

"Ha!" she said, pointing at Kip, who was perched on the counter with his front legs curled under him. "A cat in the kitchen. I knew it."

"That's not a cat," Bonnie said in a stage whisper. "That's my new sous chef. Be careful what you say—he's a bit self-conscious about his abundant facial hair."

Taryn smiled at the joke, feeling slightly more hopeful if Bonnie was back to teasing. She reached out and touched Bonnie, running her finger along the vee of her shirt, from collarbone down. "I missed you," she said, closing her eyes with relief when she felt Bonnie's hands settle on her waist. Relief turned to something much stronger when Bonnie tugged her closer, but Taryn was more than ready to handle this.

Bonnie rested her forehead against Taryn's. "Do you still want us to go slow?"

Taryn's answer was to press Bonnie against the edge of the counter, molding them together along the lengths of their bodies. "Slow didn't seem to work too well for us," she said, shifting her hips against Bonnie's. "Maybe we should try a different speed?" She slid her fingers into Bonnie's hair and moved forward until their lips met. The intensity she had felt before was still there, growing like a swelling wave as their kiss deepened from the almost chaste one they had shared before into something much more relentless. This time, though, Taryn didn't fight her response to the heat of Bonnie's mouth on hers, or the feel of her hands sliding under the hem of Taryn's top and pressing against her lower back, or the buzzing sound in her…

They pulled away from each other slightly as Isa came in the kitchen.

"Isa, get out," Bonnie said.

"The timer's going off. You told me to get the quiches out of the oven."

Taryn sniffed, suddenly aware of the cheesy aroma in the room. "Ooh, quiche. Yum."

Bonnie sighed. "Okay, take the quiches out of the oven, and then get out."

Isa crossed the kitchen and turned off the timer. "If you two are going to be kissing in here from now on, I expect a raise."

Bonnie looked at Taryn, their eyes only inches apart. "Well? Are we?"

Taryn grinned, closing the distance between them. "Oh yes. And you'd better make it a big raise."

CHAPTER TWENTY-ONE

Taryn peered around the kitchen door. "Hurry," she said. "They're about to start."

Bonnie took off her oven mitts and tossed them on the counter, checking to make sure nothing was in danger of burning over the next few minutes, before she followed Isa and Jerome out to where they stood behind the counter. She felt a momentary, habitual desire to remain hidden in the kitchen where she stood no chance of becoming another viral meme, but she pushed that urge aside with little trouble. She walked up behind Taryn, wrapped her arms around her middle, and held her close.

"I can't believe how gorgeous it looks in here," Isa whispered, and Bonnie had to agree.

The main room was transformed by the simple color scheme. Glittery wands with ribbons and feathers attached were scattered around the room so the guests could play with the cats. The silver-trimmed and velvet beds looked like royal cat thrones rather than the much-loved, scruffy beds Bonnie knew were underneath the fabric.

Jerome and Isa had hung fairy lights around the room, high enough so the cats couldn't reach them. Multicolored cats were everywhere, wandering among the chairs and hopping onto vacant laps. Bonnie had even managed to get purple sequined bowties on a few of the calmer ones. The few members of the press that had been invited were being politely unobtrusive, and most of the time Bonnie couldn't tell them apart from the other formally dressed guests.

And in the center of the room, Marty and Lex stood facing each other and looking rather ridiculously in love. And Kip was there, too, sitting on Marty's shoe and cleaning a paw.

"Oh, look," Taryn breathed out the words, turning her head to look at Bonnie. "You taught him to stand at the altar just like I asked. You're a miracle worker."

"I am," Bonnie agreed. "I think I'm going to take some of the cats and hit the road. In performances all across the country, my cats will stand places. Unless they don't want to, of course, and then they'll walk around. Or sit. It's really rather hard to predict, but it will be an impressive show."

Taryn laughed quietly, looking back at the scene as Marty and Lex spoke their vows. "Kip might not be available for the tour. I have a feeling you'll be getting an adoption request for him soon."

"I've already got the forms ready to go. I took him off the list of available cats right after the tasting back in the spring. I figured it was only a matter of time before Lex and Marty came back for him."

Taryn covered Bonnie's arms with hers and pulled them closer around her. "I should have brought Sasha and Ninja Cat. They would have loved to see this."

"We'll show them the video later. I'll make popcorn."

Isa leaned toward them. "While the image of a cat happily eating a bowl of popcorn might be a charming one, movie theater food is not a healthy option for them."

Taryn covered her mouth to muffle her laughter, but Bonnie just shook her head. "Aren't you graduating soon?" she asked. "Maybe looking for another job?"

"Not soon, but when I do, you're going to hire me as your business partner."

"Doubtful," said Bonnie, but she felt Taryn squeeze her hands, and she responded by gripping hers in return. They had been talking about Bonnie offering Isa a more permanent position at the café, but Bonnie had worried she wouldn't be interested. She was already managing most of the accounts, and the added help would give Bonnie time to work on other projects. Apparently, Isa was applying for and offering herself the job in one time-saving action. She was efficient, Bonnie would give her that.

They fell silent as they watched the rest of the ceremony. When it was finished, a friend of Marty and Lex's played the guitar and sang. None of the cats joined in, but the café's newest resident stood on her hind legs behind him the entire time, batting at his guitar strap.

"That's adorable," Taryn said, pulling out her phone and taking a picture. "I'm sending this to your parents, so they can see their newest grandbaby."

Bonnie rubbed her forehead but didn't try to stop her. Her attempts would fail, anyway.

She had brought Taryn to a family barbecue during the summer, where Taryn had talked happily about the fact that between the two of them, she and Bonnie had given Bonnie's parents thirty-two grandchildren, the largest family of anyone there. She then proceeded to tell them stories about each individual grandcat. Jonah thought she was brilliant, and by the end of the evening, he and Mayu had hired her to plan their vow renewal, which they were now determined to hold in the cat café.

Bonnie let go of Taryn's waist but kept hold of her hand as the guests stood up and started to mingle. The food was ready to serve, and everyone—human and feline—seemed relaxed and happy. It seemed to be the perfect chance to sneak away, just for a few stolen moments.

She tugged on Taryn's hand, leading her into the recently completed addition. The kitten residents were in the upstairs room for the night, as promised to Lex and Marty, but they lived in the tearooms now. Bonnie was able to serve twice as many guests because of the separate rooms—and rescue twice as many kittens—but she was still booked out months in advance. She and Taryn were living in her rental house still, because they couldn't fit themselves, four cats, and one growing kitten into the main suite. Bonnie didn't care where they slept or lived, as long as they were all together.

The moon was shining brightly through the big picture windows, so they left the lights out and sat on the window seat. They rested back against the cushions.

"I knew it was going to change my life," Bonnie said, turning her head to brush her lips across Taryn's hair. "When I said yes to you, and yes to having the wedding here. At the time, I thought that was a dangerous thing, but I can't imagine going back to the way I was before you."

"We couldn't go back, even if we tried," Taryn said. "We're too connected now. Us, our cats, our lives. Even our jobs are intersecting in some ways. Remember the day I came back to adopt Sasha and Ninja Cat? They were sleeping, all jumbled together in the basket by the window. I couldn't tell where one began and the other left off. That's us now."

Bonnie smiled and kissed Taryn's neck. "I like that."

"So," Taryn said, in the overly casual tone of someone who was about to ask a not-casual question. "The wedding was beautiful, wasn't it? Could you see yourself doing that someday? Getting married here?"

Bonnie felt herself go still at Taryn's question. "Can you see yourself getting married in your office?" she asked.

Taryn laughed softly. "Okay, I see your point."

"Not here," Bonnie said. "But maybe somewhere else. Ben and Daisy's farm would be nice. The one you're planning there is going to be wonderful. Or a garden somewhere, like the one I've shown you around the corner."

Taryn nodded. "A garden sounds lovely. The perfumed air and buzzing bees."

"Yes," Bonnie agreed. There was no perfume in the air tonight, but she felt a sense of expectancy surrounding them. "You plan weddings based on what matters most to the people involved, so if I hired you, I would only have one request. That you would be the one I'm marrying."

Taryn snuggled deeper into her arms. "You're the only one I'd want to marry, too," she said, turning her head to kiss Bonnie. She leaned away slightly. "As long as Ninja Cat gets to be best man, of course."

"I wouldn't have it any other way," Bonnie said with a laugh as she pulled Taryn into another kiss.

About the Author

Karis Walsh is a horseback riding instructor who lives in the Pacific Northwest. When she isn't teaching or writing, she enjoys spending time outside with her animals, reading, playing the viola, and riding with friends.

Books Available From Bold Strokes Books

Catch by Kris Bryant. Convincing the wife of the star quarterback to walk away from her family was never in offensive coordinator Sutton McCoy's game plan. But standing on the sidelines when a second chance at true love comes her way proves all but impossible. (978-1-63679-276-7)

Hearts in the Wind by MJ Williamz. Beth and Evelyn seem destined to remain mortal enemies but are about to discover that in matters of the heart, sometimes you must cast your fortunes to the wind. (978-1-63679-288-0)

Hero Complex by Jesse J. Thoma. Bronte, Athena, and their unlikely friends must work together to defeat Bronte's archnemesis. The fate of love, humanity, and the world might depend on it. No pressure. (978-1-63679-280-4)

Hotel Fantasy by Piper Jordan. Molly Taylor has a fantasy in mind that only Lexi can fulfill. However, convincing her to participate could prove challenging. (978-1-63679-207-1)

Last New Beginning by Krystina Rivers. Can commercial broker Skye Kohl and contractor Bailey Kaczmarek overcome their pride and work together while the tension between them boils over into a love that could soothe both of their hearts? (978-1-63679-261-3)

Love and Lattes by Karis Walsh. Cat café owner Bonnie and wedding planner Taryn join forces to get rescue cats into forever homes—discovering their own forever along the way. (978-1-63679-290-3)

Repatriate by Jaime Maddox. Ally Hamilton's new job as a home health aide takes an unexpected twist when she discovers a fortune in stolen artwork and must repatriate the masterpieces and avoid the wrath of the violent man who stole them. (978-1-63679-303-0)

The Hues of Me and You by Morgan Lee Miller. Arlette Adair and Brooke Dawson almost fell in love in college. Years later, they unexpectedly run into each other and come face-to-face with their unresolved past. (978-1-63679-229-3)

A Haven for the Wanderer by Jenny Frame. When Griffin Harris comes to Rosebrook village, the love she finds with Bronte de Lacey creates a safe haven and she finally finds her place in the world. But will she run again when their love is tested? (978-1-63679-291-0)

A Spark in the Air by Dena Blake. Internet executive Crystal Tucker is sure Wi-Fi could really help small-town residents, even if it means putting an internet café out of business, but her instant attraction to the owner's daughter, Janie Elliott, makes moving ahead with her plans complicated. (978-1-63679-293-4)

Between Takes by CJ Birch. Simone Lavoie is convinced her new job as an intimacy coordinator will give her a fresh perspective. Instead, problems on set and her growing attraction to actress Evelyn Harper only add to her worries. (978-1-63679-309-2)

Camp Lost and Found by Georgia Beers. Nobody knows better than Cassidy and Frankie that life doesn't always give you what you want. But sometimes, if you're lucky, life gives you exactly what you need. (978-1-63679-263-7)

Fire, Water, and Rock by Alaina Erdell. As Jess and Clare reveal more about themselves, and their hot summer fling tips over into true love, they must confront their pasts before they can contemplate a future together. (978-1-63679-274-3)

Lines of Love by Brey Willows. When even the Muse of Love doesn't believe in forever, we're all in trouble. (978-1-63555-458-8)

Only This Summer by Radclyffe. A fling with Lily promises to be exactly what Chase is looking for—short-term, hot as a forest fire, and one Chase can extinguish whenever she wants. After all, it's only one summer. (978-1-63679-390-0)

Picture-Perfect Christmas by Charlotte Greene. Two former rivals compete to capture the essence of their small mountain town at Christmas, all the while fighting old and new feelings. (978-1-63679-311-5)

Playing Love's Refrain by Lesley Davis. Drew Dawes had shied away from the world of music until Wren Banderas gave her a reason to play their love's refrain. (978-1-63679-286-6)